THE LIES OF KITTY BENNET

A PRIDE AND PREJUDICE VARIATION

AMANDA ORNECK

GOLD LEAF BOOKS

ISBN: 978-0-9968435-4-6 (Paperback)

ISBN: 978-0-9968435-5-3 (Ebook)

Editing by Diana Bright

Cover design by Uvarova Mariia

First printing edition 2025

Gold Leaf Books

115 Spirit Drive

Toney, Alabama 35773

www.goldleafbooks.com

amanda.orneck.com

For every Kitty out there; the second, third, and even fourth sisters.
May you all step out into the sunshine.

PROLOGUE

*D*earest Lydia,

I was absolutely delighted to hear all about the officer's ball. How splendid you must have looked in all your finery! It is such a comfort to know that, even though you are simply miles away, you still find ways to draw me into your thrilling world.

Worry not about me, dearest sister. Things at Longbourn have settled quite peacefully since Mary's wedding. The send-off to Oxford was nothing like one might expect for such a staid prude of a woman, but her new husband, Mr. Thorn, seems positively impatient to return to his studies. So eager to bury himself in work—can you fathom it? It defies all understanding! As for me, I have been utterly plagued by the worst bout of sneezing yet. With the spring winds in Meryton growing fiercer, I am reduced to a watering pot nearly every hour of the day.

But enough of this dull chatter—I have exciting news of my own! Papa was feeling unaccountably cheery during Mary's wedding breakfast, pulled me aside with a most astonishing proclamation. He wishes to see me married to a gentleman even grander than Mary's Mr. Thorn. To that end, he has promised me a dowry of one thousand pounds to attract a suitable match. Is that not drole? I an heiress! Who would have thought Kitty Bennet would amount to so much!

I do hope we might visit Bath this summer. How glorious it would be to dance in a proper assembly room! Wouldn't that be simply perfect?

Do write soon and tell me all about your adventures. I am simply dying to hear from you. I miss you terribly.

Your,
Kitty

Kitty Bennet stared down at the ink as it dried on the page, a jolt of shock mingling with delight at her own audacity. Until now, her fibs had been trifling—small embellishments that painted her as wittier in conversation or altered an assembly's events to cast her in a better light among the local girls. But this fib about the dowry—this was her boldest yet, her most outrageous act of deception. Folding the letter carefully, she savored the thrill of her secret, one meant only for Lydia. A secret that would never come true.

Yet Kitty knew precisely who she was. The last of the Bennet sisters to remain unwed. The sister everyone expected to stay behind, to tend to their aging parents. But where would that home be, she wondered? When Papa passed, they would all be tossed out on their ear by Charlotte Lucas and Mr. Collins. Still, Kitty reassured herself, such troubles were for Mama to face, and they were years away yet.

Her concerns were of a different sort entirely. These days, her greatest struggle was staving off the crushing monotony of Meryton life. Nothing ever changed here, and she was fairly certain there would be no grand excursion to Bath to search for a suitor. What would be the point without a dowry? She was already on the shelf, after all.

Kitty's shortcomings haunted her. She lacked the wit of Lizzy, the beauty of Jane, the intellect of Mary, and the uncontainable charm of Lydia. Her plainness stood in stark relief against the glow of her sisters, and she felt its weight more acutely with each passing day. Spinsterhood loomed large in her future. But in her letters to Lydia, she could escape. She could stretch the truth, just a little. And really, where was the harm in that?

CHAPTER ONE

MARCH, 1815

K itty always had the same breakfast. It was Lydia's breakfast—a choice her sister had claimed from the modest spread on the sideboard at Longbourn. A cup of overly sweetened tea, a slice of toast slathered with marmalade, and a single piece of undercooked bacon. Kitty despised marmalade, yet every morning, the upstairs maid set it before her the moment she sat down in her customary seat at the dining table. It seemed that even Lydia's absence had a way of lingering.

Not much had changed for Kitty since her sisters had married and embarked on their own adventures. She still occupied the same chair at the table she always had as the fourth Bennet sister, though the dining room now felt cavernous without the chatter and lively quips of her older siblings. The absence of their voices left a hollow silence, broken only by Mrs. Bennet's endless stream of commentary—a performance that, mercifully, never wavered.

"I know Sister Phillips was kind enough to gift us the Chantilly lace from her last trip to Devonshire," Mrs. Bennet declared, her voice rising as though addressing a crowded room, "but I must say it clashes most horribly with the pattern on the drawing room walls. Do you not agree, Mr. Bennet?"

"I fail to see how lace can clash with wallpaper, my bride," Mr. Bennet replied, his tone rich with amusement. "If the design offends you, why not simply focus on the holes rather than the whole?" He punctuated his jest with a satisfied bite of kippers, his eyes gleaming with quiet triumph.

Kitty thought her father rather clever, though not nearly as clever as he believed himself to be.

Her mother, meanwhile, wrinkled her delicate features in puzzlement. "Holes and holes? Whatever can you mean, Mr. Bennet? You must be troubled by some difficulty on the farm. Are there gophers in the stableyard again?" Shaking her curls with a tut of disapproval, she resumed eating her toast and jam.

The butler entered quietly, carrying the morning's correspondence on a silver salver, which he placed beside Mr. Bennet's elbow. Folding his newspaper with deliberate care, Mr. Bennet sifted through the envelopes until one, in particular, caught his eye.

"Well, Kitty," he said with a sly smile, holding up a letter, "it seems your dear Lydia has written to you."

Kitty shot to her feet, her heart leaping as she scampered eagerly down the length of the dining table. "Oh, Papa, may I read it? Please?" It had been months since she last heard from her youngest sister, and she was filled to the brim with curiosity bout Lydia's life with the regiment.

Mr. Bennet chuckled softly as he handed her the envelope. "Indeed, daughter. I only ask that you share any news of consequence." With that, he turned back to the pile of correspondence, selecting a letter with an unfamiliar seal. Cracking it open, he unfolded the paper and began to read.

As his eyes moved over the words, the faint smile that had lingered on his face darkened into a furrowed frown.

Kitty watched her father with the sourness of worry mixing with the overly sweet marmalade in her stomach. "Papa? Is ought amiss?"

Distracted by his reading, it took a moment for Mr. Bennet to register Kitty's question. When she repeated it, his head snapped up, positively glowering. "Yes, I would say so. I had hoped to purchase the western expanse of land adjoining our property. We need more grazing land for the cattle. Unfortunately, it seems the deal has fallen through."

He exhaled sharply, shaking the letter in his hand as though it bore the blame. "But never you mind my trials, Young Kitty. Run along, read your letter, and leave me to brood over mine." He waved her off with the offending missive.

Kitty clutched Lydia's letter to her chest, a small flutter of excitement returning despite her father's sour mood. She was just pushing back her chair, ready to retreat to the quiet of the morning room, when her mother stood abruptly, as though the preceding conversation had not occurred at all.

"Kitty," Mrs. Bennet began, her tone brisk and businesslike, "you must return this lace to Sister Phillips before you go running off with your letters. I simply cannot abide this pattern in the house a moment longer. It clashes terribly, and it sets my nerves on edge. I shall have the maids pack it up for you."

"Yes, Mama. Of course," Kitty replied, sighing inwardly but keeping her face polite. "I'll fetch my shawl and bonnet." With a practiced motion, she slipped the unopened letter into her pocket where it sat alongside her disappointment. The trip to Meryton to visit her Aunt Phillips would only take an hour or so. Then, she promised herself, she would find a quiet spot and finally uncover Lydia's news. A little patience was all she needed.

With her outdoor trappings retrieved and donned, Kitty stood in the foyer, waiting for several minutes for her mother to appear. She was just considering whether she had enough time to read her letter before the trip to town when Mrs. Bennet bounced into view, a large, flat parcel in her hands.

"Now mind you don't wrinkle the lace," her mother instructed, her voice sharp with authority. "Carry it in both hands and don't set it down anywhere but in Sister Phillips' hands."

"Yes, Mama," Kitty replied in her most submissive tone. Mrs. Bennet bustled her out the door and into the sunshine without another word.

Kitty paused for a moment, blinking at the garden flowers, the warmth of the sun seeping into her skin, before the door clicked shut behind her. With a spring in her step and an itch in her nose, Kitty set off to complete her mother's errand. After all, obedience was the role of the last daughter still living at home. Wasn't it?

It had always been the ritual of the Bennet sisters to walk into Meryton in search of a little amusement. Most of these outings had been orchestrated by the youngest of the girls, for Lydia was ever craving something new and exciting to enliven her days. Kitty had long since lost track of the times she had trailed along in that familiar clump of sisters—always behind Mary's rigid posture, whispering and giggling with Lydia over some lark or other.

Even now, as Kitty walked alone along the well-trodden road between Longbourn and Meryton, she could almost see the ghostly shapes of her sisters ahead of her: Mary, straight-backed and proper, her stride deliberate; Lydia, her head inclined toward Kitty, eyes bright with gossip she couldn't wait to spill. The memory brought a faint smile to her lips, but it faded as quickly as it had come.

Though her steps now fell alone, it was hard not to feel as though she still walked in her accustomed place—second from last, forever trailing behind sisters who had all found their own paths. And yet here she was, Kitty Bennet, making their usual pilgrimage to the village on her own. The thought settled heavily upon her, slowing her steps as though the weight of it pressed down upon her shoulders.

She was now the last Miss Bennet, but it never felt as though she was *the* Miss Bennet—not in the way that Jane had been with her beauty or Lizzy with her wit. Even Mary had carried herself with a certain moral conviction, however tedious. And now, of course, they were all happily married—even Mary, whose heart had once seemed so firmly closed to any notion of romance. Well, romance that did not involve Mr. Collins, at least.

Kitty wouldn't follow in their footsteps. How could she? Hertfordshire offered little society to a young woman like her, and even if it had, there were her parents to consider. They would need her support as the years weighed heavier upon them. No, Kitty Bennet would remain the last Miss Bennet—and she would find a way to be content with her lot.

Reaching the outskirts of town, Kitty adjusted the parcel of lace on her forearms, holding it as carefully as a butler might present a tray of sweetmeats at a dinner party. Her mother had placed the package there with deliberate precision, and Kitty was certain she was expected to maintain this posture until the parcel was safely delivered to her aunt's hands.

It was a small mercy that the Phillips family resided on the west side of Meryton, their neat little townhouse nestled along a quiet side street that meandered from the edge of town toward the river. But as the house came into view, two difficulties presented themselves.

The first obstacle was the picket fence, draped in fragrant drifts of pink roses, its quaint charm somewhat marred by the gate standing resolutely shut. Kitty paused, considering her options. The parcel rested precariously on her forearms, and the thought of shifting it sent a shiver of apprehension through her. Deciding against disturbing her burden, she shifted her weight onto one leg and nudged the gate with her foot.

The gate resisted.

She nudged it again, a little harder this time. Still, it wouldn't budge.

On the third attempt, Kitty summoned all the vigor she could manage, delivering a sharp and decisive kick. The gate finally yielded with a creak of protest, swinging open just wide enough for her to slip through.

The second obstacle was the front door, which also stood resolutely closed. Kitty, feeling it improper to apply her booted foot to the surface of her uncle's home, adjusted the package so it balanced in the crook of her elbow. With her unoccupied hand, she gave a series of polite knocks upon the door.

When the door finally opened, it was Maisy, the housemaid, who stood within.

"Good morning, Maisy. I am come to visit my Aunt Phillips. Can you let her know I am here?"

Maisy nodded her assent and, with a curtsy, ushered Kitty inside.

Kitty always loved how quiet the Phillips' house was, a marked contrast to the riotous atmosphere she had been raised in at Longbourn. Mrs. Phillips spent much of her time engaged in womanly pursuits, such as painting or embroidery, and the peaceful, contemplative air she exuded was something Kitty greatly appreciated. It was a welcome change from the bustle and endless chatter of her own home.

However, today, Mrs. Phillips appeared anything but tranquil as she hurried down the stairs from the first-floor apartments.

"Kitty, darling! How marvelous to see you!" she exclaimed. "I so wish I had time to sit down for a nice cose but we are due for a guest to arrive at any moment. I am at sixes and sevens trying to figure out how to accommodate him in our tiny abode."

It must be said that the home Mrs. Phillips considered so minuscule had no less than three bedrooms, a parlor, and a book room, all neatly arranged in a small park that boasted a lovely cut-flower garden in the front and a practical kitchen garden in the back. It should also be noted that Mrs. Phillips shared her sister's tendency to exaggerate.

"I am sorry not to be able to spend time with you, Aunt," Kitty said, though she truly felt no regret at all. She had just remembered the letter sitting unread in her pocket. "But I wouldn't want to inconvenience you for the world. I have brought a package from my mother and will be happy to leave it and be on my way."

"Thank you, dear. You are always so accommodating," Mrs. Phillips replied, her smile warm. "Maisy can take the parcel," which she did with another curtsy, "and I shall return to my chaos."

"Who is visiting you, Aunt, if you don't mind my asking?" Kitty inquired, her curiosity piqued.

"I must admit he might not be a guest so much as an employee, but it amounts to the same thing in the end. A new clerk has come to train under Mr. Phillips at the law firm, and he will be residing with us. I only hope he isn't a rattle. You know how I hate jabber at the dinner table."

Kitty smiled and nodded politely, not trusting herself to reply. Mrs. Phillips led her to the door, opened it, and kissed her goodbye. "Au revoir, dear Kitty. Stop by again soon, and I will tell you all the news about our new lodger. All I know at this point is that his name is Tiffin, and he's from Cumbria of all places. Just imagine!"

Kitty's smile stretched into a grin as her aunt waved her off and closed the door. It seemed Aunt Phillips considered Cumbria to be quite the ends of the earth.

Kitty stepped down from the stoop of the Phillips' townhouse, her hand already slipping into her pocket. There was a lovely reading spot in her aunt's garden that would be perfect for Lydia's letter. But as she approached the corner of the house where the garden began, she heard her name called.

Mariah Lucas was walking down the road, and with a wave, she approached the Phillips' gate. "Why, beloved Kitty, how pleasant to see you! I was just thinking of you as I walked to town. I have something to purchase for my mother. Would you join me?"

Kitty did not want to join Mariah. She had nothing against her friend, only her timing. It seemed the world was conspiring with all the citizens of Meryton to keep Kitty from Lydia's letter. Still, it had been some days since she had spoken with Mariah, and it was always pleasant to spend time with her.

Kitty and Mariah were in a similar position and of a similar age. They were both the last remaining unmarried daughters of their respective households, both teetering on the precipice of spinsterhood. Kitty did not expect Mariah to remain unwed for long, not with her dark beauty and charming poise. In that respect, they were not alike at all. Kitty knew, in her heart of hearts, that she herself was destined to join the ranks of the ape leaders.

And so, she smiled up at her friend and opened the gate. "I would love to."

Mariah spoke of small nothings as they walked. "Is your family well?"

Kitty nodded. "They are, although there seems to be some small problem with my father's purchase of land near Longbourn. I don't quite understand the issue, but he seemed most put out when I left."

"That is a shame," Mariah said, wrinkling her pale brow in concern. "I hope he solves the problem swiftly."

"Thank you."

"And your aunt?" It was known by most in town that the best news always came from Aunt Phillips.

"She is expecting a guest at any moment and could not speak with me, so unfortunately, I have nothing new to relate."

This piqued Mariah's interest. "A new guest, you say?"

"Yes, a Mr. Tiffin from Cumbria. He will evidently be beginning employment under Mr. Phillips at the law practice here in Meryton." Kitty watched Mariah's dark eyes shine with growing curiosity.

"A young man? Single, I suppose?" Ah, there it was—Mariah's desire for a beau. Kitty should have expected it.

"I cannot say, but she did not mention a wife. I would assume that he would be traveling with his family, should he have one, don't you think?"

"Did she say anything else? About his looks, perhaps, or his tastes?" Mariah leaned in eagerly, grasping Kitty's arm in her desire to know more.

Kitty laughed. "No, she only said he was coming and that she didn't have time for a chat. When I learn more, I shall be certain to illuminate you on all things Tiffin."

"You are the best of friends, Kitty Bennet." Mariah wrapped her arm around Kitty's, and together they headed into the heart of Meryton toward the grand church at its center. Mariah was looking for pen nibs for her mother's correspondence, and once they were purchased, the two girls wandered back the way they had come.

Mariah left Kitty at the gate to the Phillips' townhouse with a handshake. "Remember to call on me the minute you have news. You are sworn to this vow, so remember now."

Kitty nodded. "All things Tiffin. As soon as I know something, you will find me at your door." She waved Mariah off and turned to look longingly at the garden. There was time yet before she was expected home. Surely there were a few moments to spare. She could enter the house and meet the new lodger, for she heard conversation muffled through the sitting room windows, or... Kitty's heart quickened. Or she could sit under that lovely maple tree and finally read Lydia's letter. Stepping into the garden, she pulled the letter from her pocket and sighed with happiness as she finally began to read.

Isaac Tiffin was out of his depth. He knew it the moment he stepped out of the mail coach into the bustling din that was Meryton, Herefordshire. First, he nearly collided with the coachman as he pulled the luggage from its perch atop the conveyance. Next, he trod on the edge of a lady's cloak as he attempted to help her descend. It was truly an inauspicious beginning to his new life, and he could not help but take it as a sign of things to come.

Awash in a sea of humanity and road dust, it took Isaac several moments to hear his name being called from somewhere within the crowded stableyard of the inn. Finally, he heard "Tiffin!" accompanied by a waving beaver, and made the assumption that he should head in that direction. As the crowd parted, Isaac saw the figure of a well-dressed man smiling from beneath his greying whiskers, replacing his hat atop his thinning hair.

"Tiffin?" The man inquired, looking up at Isaac with pale, inquiring eyes.

"I am Isaac Tiffin, sir. Might you be Mr. Phillips?"

The smile broadened into a grin. "That I am, my boy. I welcome you to Meryton. How was your journey? Not too bad, I hope?"

"I've an aching back from the cramped coach, and the bumps in the road were torture on my head. I can still feel the jostling at the back of my skull."

Mr. Phillips' eyebrows rose as he surveyed Isaac's bulk. It seemed likely the man himself would get a neckache from staring up at him. "I am sorry your journey was so uncomfortable. Let's get you to Mrs. Phillips and a cup of tea right quick, eh?"

"Tea? If we must," Isaac replied without thinking, then regretted his usual bluntness. This was no way to impress an employer, especially one who had done so much for his Grannie Tiffin. Out of his depth indeed.

The Phillips household was a fine townhouse a few blocks from the main road, and Mr. Phillips remained quiet during their walk, which gave Isaac just enough time to worry about what was to come. He had never been in a town larger than his village, beyond a yearly trip to York, and that had always scared him so much that he stayed near his cart until his goods were sold and left as soon as he was able, never mind being on the road home in the dark. Meryton was a pretty little town with a great, large church at its center, and the spokes of the town's streets spread out like a wheel from that grand edifice. The roads were neatly cobbled, which also reminded Isaac of York. All this organized gentility set his teeth on edge.

Stepping inside the townhouse, Isaac had to duck to avoid hitting the doorframe, turning sideways so his broad shoulders could fit. He felt as if he were a tin soldier forced into a dollhouse built for toys half his size. A woman bustled forward from the depths of the house. She folded her hands primly before her and smiled up at him, though the smile faltered as she realized just how high she had to look to meet Isaac's face.

"Why, hello there, you must be Mr. Tiffin. Welcome! I am Mrs. Phillips, and I am most happy to have you staying with our family. Would you like me to show you to your room first, or shall we have some tea?" Mrs. Phillips managed to set her smile back in place, and her voice carried warmth and openness.

Still, Isaac couldn't shake the feeling of being a giant in such a delicate house, surrounded by fine gold mirrors and flower vases perched on plinths in the foyer. Just the thought of moving in such a space made him uneasy, knowing that the slightest misstep could send them crashing to the parquet.

"Hallo, ma'am. I am happy to be here. I don't need to see a room at the moment. Wherever you have me put is fine. I were used to sleeping in the hayloft during the summers, so if you've got a spare bit of straw in the stables, that'd suit me perfectly."

Isaac stopped speaking when he noticed Mrs. Phillips' smile falter again.

"The stables? Heaven forfend!" Mrs. Phillips exclaimed. "No guest of mine will be sleeping with the stable lad in the mews. I have a tidy little room on the third floor, next to the male staff."

"Granted, my boy," her husband added with a grin, "you might hear enough snoring through the walls to make it sound like you're sleeping with the horses."

He led Isaac into a very well-appointed sitting room, gestured to a chair, and bade him sit.

Isaac lowered himself into the armchair as gently as he could, his broad shoulders too wide to allow him to settle comfortably. *Calm down, man,* he chided himself. *You canna lose a job the same day you arrive. You've got to be polite, like.*

A few minutes of awkward silence passed before the housekeeper bustled in with the tea things. Mrs. Phillips took center stage, pouring out tea into delicate cups.

"Cream? Sugar?" "Nah, tea is tea. I don't need any trimmings," Isaac grumbled under the weight of his discomfort. His hostess nodded and handed him the plain cup. It took all his focus not to crack the fine china as he took a sip. Was everything in this new life of his delicate and fragile like this cup? How would he ever survive the week, much less his entire life, if he was in constant fear of breaking something or offending someone? *Grannie Tiffin, what am I to do?* Isaac drank his tea and tried to focus as he was bombarded with the same questions he had already answered for Mr. Phillips. How was the journey? "Long." Would he miss Cumbria? "Of course." He must be grieving his grandmother terribly. Was there anything they could do? "Losses happen to everyone."

He was nearly out of patience when a stiff breeze rattled the windows of the sitting room. Then, a mighty sneeze echoed from somewhere nearby. Isaac couldn't help but commiserate with the sneezer. He too was uncomfortable, bothered by something that made his insides itch. If only he could banish the invasive questions the way a sneeze chased away irritants from one's nose.

Alas, he was trapped, far from everything he knew, away from the calm of life outdoors, forced to sit in a highly-breakable chair and hold a highly-breakable cup until his highly-breakable spirit, too, was on the verge of shattering. Was there nothing in all of Herefordshire that could save him from this torment?

Stepping into the garden, Kitty made her way to the beloved bench beneath the maple tree and finally broke the seal on her sister's letter.

Dearest Kitty,

I cannot tell you what joy I felt when I heard the news that Papa had provided a dowry for our own little Kitty. What a lark! To think that our father, who once begrudged every farthing when we asked for pin money for trimmings or a new bonnet – that man eagerly opened his wallet to see his last daughter wed!

La! I laughed for a full ten minutes when I read that, and so did Wickham when I shared the letter with him. You know how busy he is, but this time, he actually put down his paper and coffee to read your words – what a loving brother-in-law you have, Kitty!

When he read of your good fortune, he laughed too, though it wasn't long before he became rather cross. You may recall, or perhaps you never knew, how hard poor Wickham had it after our marriage. I can tell you that Papa did very little in the way of wedding presents, even though I was the first of his daughters to marry – and the youngest, at that!

In any case, before I go on, I simply must tell you about a visit we had from Wickham's cousin—

At that moment, several things occurred all at once. First, a breeze stirred, carrying the scent of freshly mown grass from the townhouse next door. Unfortunately, the gardener had chosen that very morning to take up his scythe, and Kitty's nose always proved susceptible to the smell of newly cut grass. The breeze, laden with its intoxicating fragrance, made her nose itch most unbearably.

Then, with a great, forceful sneeze, Kitty lost her grip on the letter. It wasn't until she blinked her watering eyes, struggling to clear them, that she realized what had happened. She glanced down in horror, only to see the wretched Spring breeze, laden with grass, whisking her letter away down the street.

Isaac Tiffin sat in uncomfortable silence in the Phillips' sitting room, wishing fervently to be anywhere but there. The tea in his cup had long since cooled, and though he was well aware of this, he felt no inclination for a second cup. Nor did he want to risk making a stain upon Mrs. Phillips' fine cherry furniture. Instead of setting the saucer down, he awkwardly clutched it in hands far too large for anything so delicate as china.

He cast a longing glance toward the sitting room window, where it seemed the spring day itself had become his co-conspirator. A gust of wind blew past, carrying with it what looked like a piece of recently folded paper. It was exactly the sign he needed.

Isaac rose, handed his half-empty tea to his hostess, and muttered something about wanting to see the outside of the house. He didn't recall the exact words, only that, in a few strides, he was out of the cramped sitting room and into the warm spring sunshine, nearly laughing with relief of it.

Surveying the area around him, Isaac's gaze was caught by movement. His paper quarry danced in the breeze, drifting toward a row of poplars along the street. Isaac jogged out of the gate, down the street, and with one long stretch of his arm, snatched the parchment before it could tangle in the tree branches.

"Whose are you, I wonder?" he muttered to the paper. It was evidently a letter, judging by the slanting, nearly illegible script that crowded one side of the page. Rather than risk accidentally reading its contents, Isaac turned the letter over to examine the recipient's name. "Kitty Bennet" was written there in the same attrocious handwriting.

He was pondering the curious nature of women's names when a loud sneeze echoed from the direction of the townhouse he had just exited. A spring breeze, a sneeze, and a letter in flight—these seemed to be connected, and Isaac followed the clues around the corner of the Phillips' townhouse into their garden. There, on a bench, he saw a woman with her bonnet askew, her eyes watering terribly. Another sneeze erupted from her little red nose, and Isaac felt a deep sympathy for her.

Reaching into his coat pocket, Isaac withdrew his handkerchief. For a moment, he hesitated, reluctant to offer the rough homespun fabric to a lady, but it was clear she needed assistance, and this was all he could provide.

"Here, miss." He proffered the handkerchief, and she accepted it with a wan smile. Blowing her nose and wiping her eyes, she looked up at him gratefully, then leaned back slightly to get a better view of his face.

Here it comes, Isaac silently braced himself for the shock he knew would follow. He had grown accustomed to it, after all—why he had spent most of his days on the farm, only venturing into York when necessary to sell wool or meat. His shoulders huddled in anticipation of the reactions he had learned to expect: polite shock, or, if they were bolder, open derision. Being a man of his size, Isaac was no stranger to mockery, and he braced himself for it.

"Oh!" the young woman began. Isaac nearly winced, wishing to flee before she finished the sentence, but instead, she asked, "Is that my letter?"

Isaac glanced down at his left hand, which still held the wayward letter. He had completely forgotten about it in the midst of meeting the young lady.

"Er, yes, I saw it fly away and thought I might as well catch it before a tree tore it to shreds," he explained, handing the letter over to her. She accepted it with her free hand, now holding both his offerings.

"Thank you!" she grinned up at him, her voice cracking slightly as she spoke around her sniffles. She shoved the letter into a hidden compartment in her gown, adding, "I thought I'd lost it forever, and I hadn't even had a chance to finish reading it. What a savior you are!"

Isaac ducked his head, feeling a strange warmth at the praise. "No need for all the thanks, it's just a bit of paper." He hesitated, unsure why it felt so odd to be on the receiving end of kindness instead of mockery. Didn't she notice his height? His giant build?

Eager to change the subject, Isaac gestured toward the handkerchief still in her hand. "You can keep that, but you shouldn't be out on breezy days with such a bad case of summer asthma. Best to stay indoors and keep a damp cloth nearby. Hasn't anyone taught you better?"

Isaac could have kicked himself for his blunt outburst, but it bothered him to see such a kind young lady suffering.

"No, I don't think they have. I've never heard of summer asthma. Is that why I sneeze when they harvest the wheat?" she asked, her voice still a bit nasally.

Isaac nodded. "My Grannie Tiffin had it something terrible, especially in the spring when the trees begin to leaf out."

"Tiffin... Does that mean you are Mr. Tiffin, the new clerk at Mr. Phillips' law practice?"

"I am, and you're Kitty Bennet, the young lady who reads letters out of doors when she ought to be inside."

A tinkling laugh bubbled up from her, soft and melodic. It was the prettiest sound Isaac had ever heard.

"I think you are very wise, Mr. Tiffin, and I'm very glad you've come here," she said, smiling warmly. "I will follow your advice and go find a damp cloth for my summer asthma." She stood, curtsied, and left the garden, heading north up the street.

Isaac watched until she disappeared from view. Never had he been called wise before, and for some reason, he found he quite liked it. In fact, he liked it very much indeed.

CHAPTER TWO

Kitty wandered home with a light heart, her steps punctuated by occasional sneezes and spontaneous smiles. How kind Mr. Tiffin had been! He was the first person ever to offer insight into her incessant sneezing. For years, she had simply listened to Dr. Margraves, accepting his diagnosis that her humours were out of balance, meekly enduring his occasional application of leeches.

But Mr. Tiffin, with his quiet certainty, had explained it was not a weakness of her blood, but summer asthma! Kitty could scarcely contain her excitement. She would have to ask him, when they next met, why a complaint meant for summer should arise in the spring. That was a puzzle she wasn't equipped to solve.

Lost in her musings, she was still smiling when she rounded the corner of Longbourn and saw something unusual—a sleek black carriage, unfamiliar and grand, standing in the drive. John the footman was stacking luggage onto the front steps, his movements brisk.

"Who's arrived, John?" Kitty asked, her curiosity piqued.

"Not sure, miss," John replied with his usual respectful tone, though his eyes gleamed with the pride of someone who fancied himself a butler-in-training. "But I've never seen him before. Very fancy, I'll tell you that."

An unknown gentleman, and a fancy one at that? Kitty's intrigue deepened. She stepped inside the foyer, pulled off her bonnet, and placed it carefully on the peg reserved for such things. From the morning room, she heard her mother's unmistakable chortling, a sound that suggested whatever guest had arrived was already on good terms with her. That was something, at least.

Kitty took a deep breath, trying to calm the sudden onset of nerves, before stepping through the door to the morning room.

Three figures were inside. Her parents sat up straight on the settee, and across from them was a stranger of dark mien and striking appearance.

"Kitty!" her mother squealed, her voice infused with more enthusiasm than Kitty had ever heard focused in her direction. "Wherever have you been?"

"I went to deliver the lace to Aunt Phillips, Mama, as you requested."

"Never mind that! What do I care for lace?" Mrs. Bennet sprang to her feet, dragging Kitty by both hands into the center of the room. "Come meet our guest. Mr. Blackwell, this is our daughter, Kitty."

The stranger unfolded from the armchair, a charming smile spreading across his face as he came to stand before her. With an elegant bow, he introduced himself. "Rufus Blackwell, at your service, Miss Bennet."

For a moment, Kitty stood frozen, confusion clouding her thoughts. Jane wasn't here. Didn't he know? She was off, happily married to Bingley, living life to the fullest in London. Then, with a jolt, Kitty realized—*she* was Miss Bennet now, having been so since Mary's marriage some months ago. How strange the turns of life could be.

She curtsied with an awkward tilt, one she knew would likely earn her a scolding later. "Miss Kitty Bennet. Welcome to Longbourn."

Mr. Blackwell took Kitty's hand and kissed the back of it before straightening up. "Much have I heard of the beauty of the Bennet sisters, but I fear I was misled. You are breathtaking, Miss Bennet."

Kitty barely suppressed a laugh. *Her*, breathtaking? What a lark. She had always believed Lydia remained so steadfast a sister largely because standing next to Kitty made Lydia's own beauty all the more remarkable by comparison.

She lowered her head, hiding the smile that tugged at the corners of her lips. "Surely you are exaggerating, Mr. Blackwell."

For a moment, Mr. Blackwell stood before her, his dark eyes sparkling with fervor, as though ready to contradict her. But before he could speak, her father intervened.

"Well, Blackwell, you mentioned an interest in cattle? We must take a tour of the farm tomorrow, then. I would be most interested to hear your thoughts on the expansion plans I have for the grazing fields to the west."

"I would be most gratified, Mr. Bennet." Mr. Blackwell turned back to Kitty, his smile unwavering. "And Miss Bennet, might I beg a tour of the gardens afterward?"

"Of course," Kitty said, though her heart recoiled at the thought. The way Mr. Blackwell smiled reminded her of a spider seeking new prey, and she couldn't shake the feeling that, in this scenario, she was very much the fly.

Kitty longed for the solace of her room, for a respite from the ever-smiling Mr. Blackwell, but she could not make her excuses. Her parents were clearly in agreement on the importance of their guest, and she felt it would be impolite to leave. Instead, she took a seat in a chair opposite him, accepting a cup of tea from Jenny, the maid.

Her mother launched into a conversation about the joys of Meryton, and Kitty let her mind wander. It drifted to a young man with a very different way of speaking—a man who had spoken to her without flattery. Nothing Mr. Tiffin said was meant to charm her. In fact, he had almost berated her for being out on a breezy day. How refreshing it was to speak with someone so forthright, someone who spoke his mind without dressing it up in compliments. Was he always so blunt, she wondered?

"Jenny, open the window," her mother commanded. "No doubt Mr. Blackwell would like to enjoy the beautiful spring weather we're having here in Herefordshire. Where did you say you came from?"

"I was visiting my cousin and his wife in Crewe, madam. I believe you know them, Mr. and Mrs. Wickham of His Majesty's Army?"

"Lydia? You were with my darling Lydia?" Mrs. Bennet clapped her hands in delight. "Do tell me, was she well when you last saw her? Lydia's letters are so few, and I never see my beloved girl often enough."

The mention of Lydia drew Kitty's full attention back to the conversation. Wickham's cousin. Did that mean he had been visiting Wickham when Kitty's letter arrived—the one with her biggest whopper yet? She met Mr. Blackwell's gaze, and his smile, with that spidery gleam in his eyes, confirmed her suspicions. He had come for one thing: her nonexistent dowry.

Isaac Tiffin awoke the next morning feeling utterly embarrassed. He cringed at the memory of rushing out of the sitting room the day before to chase after a scrap of paper. He winced at how he had spoken to Miss Bennet, reprimanding her for venturing out into the spring sunshine. Who was he to lecture a young lady on how to behave? The mere recollection of his words made his ears burn and his cravat feel tighter around his neck.

Dressing as a town fop was difficult enough, with all the layers of coats, waistcoats, and neckerchiefs. Isaac was too large to feel comfortable in anything other than his shirtsleeves. Add to that the knowledge that he would have to walk down the street to Phillips' law office and spend his first day working inside at a desk—he couldn't help but feel miserable.

He shouldered out of his room, a space decorated with tiny furniture that seemed to have been built on half scale, and headed down to the dining room for breakfast. The night before, he had managed to stay silent at dinner, and the Phillips family had been kind enough to give him the space to keep his own counsel. But today, when he entered the dining room, Mrs. Phillips was there to greet him.

"Good morning, Mr. Tiffin! Did you sleep well?"

Direct questions were never good news for Isaac, so he merely grunted in response.

His hostess laughed. "Not a morning person? I can understand; Bernard is much the same way. Positively a grumpy bear for the first three hours of the morning. Coffee or tea?"

"Tea, please. I cannot see the point of coffee. If I wanted dirt in my water, I'd go out into the garden and grab a handful of soil." The words were out of his mouth and into the air before Isaac even realized a pot of coffee sat in front of Mrs. Phillips. He had done it again—spoken without thinking, letting the first thing that came to mind slip out.

Mrs. Phillips lifted an eyebrow as she sipped her coffee. "I quite like coffee myself, but then I learned to love it on the continent during our honeymoon. Have you traveled much?"

Isaac appreciated how smoothly Mrs. Phillips changed the subject and responded as respectfully as he could. "Until now, I've not been further than York."

The rest of the meal passed without incident. After Isaac helped himself to food from the sideboard, his thoughts turned to worries about his new employment. His only experience with lawyers had been when Mr. Phillips handled the sale of Grannie Tiffin's farm in Cumbria. It was then that Isaac discovered his grandmother wasn't Cumbrian by birth but was actually from a town called Meryton. She had often complained about the harsh northern winters, but Isaac had always assumed it was just her natural surliness—something he himself had inherited.

When he finished his meal, Isaac nodded his goodbyes to Mrs. Phillips and made his way to Mr. Phillips's office. Standing before the door, he took a deep breath to steady his nerves and then entered.

A young clerk greeted him. "Good morning, sir. How may I help you? Mr. Phillips has yet to arrive, but I expect him any moment."

"Mrs. Phillips told me her husband hates to get up in the mornings," Isaac replied curtly.

The clerk blinked in surprise. "You know the attorney's wife? Does that mean you're Mr. Tiffin, our new clerk?" The clerk studied Isaac, noting the country cut of his coat and the dull shine of his boots.

"That's me. Put me to work with whatever you need done."

"Very well, we're happy to have you. There's always work to do, and plenty of it. I'm Mr. Smith, clerk to Mr. Phillips for three years. Let me start you with something simple to ease you in." Mr. Smith, a tidy man who barely came up to Isaac's chest, turned on his heel and marched toward a row of bookcases holding stacks of files.

"Mr. Phillips would like these files gone through for discrepancies. Many were written up by the previous clerk, and he had...shortcomings," Mr. Smith said, tapping his nose significantly.

Overwhelmed but determined not to show it, Isaac sat down at an empty desk and began reading through the files. He had no idea what he was supposed to be looking for. Most of them appeared to be general land disputes, records of rental agreements, and one or two wills. Nothing stood out, and after a while, everything began to blur together. Two hours later, when Mr. Phillips finally arrived, Isaac was nursing the beginnings of a headache.

"Ah, Isaac, my boy! I'm glad to see you've gotten straight to work. Is Smith taking good care of you?" Mr. Phillips smiled paternally around the room, noting that Isaac was hunched over a desk covered in files.

"I've been put to work, sir," Isaac replied, "though I can't make heads or tails of these files. What did he mean by 'discrepancies'?"

"Perhaps we've started you on something a bit too in-depth, eh? Come on over to my office, and I'll find you something a little less... exhaustive."

Isaac stood up abruptly, knocking over the chair and sending a stack of files cascading to the floor. In his panic, he righted the chair and moved to gather the papers, only to knock over a bottle of ink in the process. Isaac grabbed the bottle and set it upright, but not before a large pool of black ink had spilled from the desk and started to spread across the floor.

"Stop!" Mr. Smith called in alarm. "You'll only make things worse. Leave it be, Tiffin! I'll have to spend hours cleaning up this mess!"

"Apologies," Isaac mumbled, dropping the papers he had already picked up. They fluttered to the ground like falling leaves.

It was all too much. He was embarrassed, angry at himself, and fairly certain he had just lost his job within the first three hours. His face reddened with mortification, and without thinking, Isaac ran out of the room, straight for the front door.

Once outside, he kept running, his legs churning beneath him. In minutes, he found himself back at the Phillips house. But, unable to face Mrs. Phillips in such a state of humiliation, he headed for the garden instead. There, he paced up and down, up and down, until he could finally make out the details of the bushes and flowers around him.

Eventually, Isaac's pacing led him to the front part of the garden, where the bench Miss Bennet had sat on the day before stood beneath a blooming tree. He sank down onto it, putting his head in his hands, wishing with all his might that he had never come to Herefordshire.

Why did he always do this? Every time an opportunity came his way, he managed to ruin it. He had spent his life working on his grandmother's farm, but when she passed, she sold it off instead of letting him take it over and continue tending to the sheep as he always had. Was he really so bad at farming that she couldn't trust him to carry on her legacy?

Now that he was in Meryton, he had thought he might finally have a chance at a fresh start. But once again, here he was—ruining everything he touched. It seemed he was born only to make mistakes.

Frustrated, Isaac reached down and grabbed handfuls of the grass beneath him. Yanking the green blades felt oddly cathartic, so he did it again and again, until his fist was full of leaves, their delicate seed heads trembling with every breath he took.

The grass reminded him of a certain lady and her summer asthma. If he were going to be fired, the least he could do was help someone in town before he packed up and left for...where? Cumbria, he supposed, though the thought of returning there turned his stomach. He would put off that decision for later.

Standing, Isaac walked around to the kitchen door and opened it. As he stepped inside, his gaze fell on the cook, who was holding court in front of a stove laden with steaming pots.

"Do you have a stillroom here?" Isaac asked, doffing his hat with one hand, careful not to bump his head against the low ceiling.

The cook turned, her wooden spoon still in hand, and gestured without a hint of interest. "Over there." Without a second glance, she returned to her work.

Isaac crossed the tiled floor, heading toward a small room filled with dried herbs and distilling tools. For the first time since arriving in Herefordshire, he felt he was in his element. He took the blades of grass, laid them carefully on a cutting board, and separated the seed heads from the leaves. Grinding them in a mortar, he felt a slight tickle in his nose as the pollen rose into the air. Reaching for a bottle on the shelf, he filled it with honey, pausing occasionally to sprinkle in the ground grass seeds.

"Ah, here you are," came Mr. Phillips' fatherly voice from the doorway. Isaac turned to see his host leaning against the doorframe, his ever-present smile on his face. "I had wondered where you ran off to."

"I'm that sorry, sir," Isaac began.

"Hush now, none of that," Mr. Phillips waved off Isaac's apology as he straightened up. "We asked a lot of you this morning; too much, I expect."

"You asked me to read, something I've been doing since before I could walk. I'd hardly call that 'too much,' er, sir."

"On your first day, analyzing files before we've even explained what we do in our practice is too much, my boy. You've been taken from your life and thrown to the wolves down here, and for that, I'm sorry. Let's start over, eh?" Mr. Phillips extended his hand with a warm smile.

Isaac stared at it, stunned. "You mean you're not firing me?"

"For spilling ink and mixing up a few files? Nay, that wouldn't be neighborly of me, now would it? No, I think we should start off slower. I'm of a mind to send you out to meet with the family of a client. Something tells me that visiting a farm would be the perfect way to introduce you to the work we do."

"You work with farms?" Isaac stoppered the bottle he was holding, needing something to occupy his hands. He wiped the glass down with a cloth, cleaning up the last droplets of honey.

"No, but we do work for farmers. Mr. Preece recently passed away, but he never delivered a copy of his updated will to me. I know he had planned to write a second will to replace the one we made years ago, but after his death, it never arrived. It should be a simple task—head up to Preece Farm, get the will from his sons, and bring it back to the office. We have a cart kept in the mews, and Daniel can saddle Mabel for you if you ask." Mr. Phillips stepped forward and handed Isaac a piece of paper.

Isaac took the paper, still a little dazed from the swift changes in his fortune. He then accepted a handshake from the older man. "Thank you, sir," he said, his gratitude deep but beyond words. Instead, he poured all his thanks into the handshake until he heard Mr. Phillips grunt in mock protest.

"Of course, my boy. Now head on out. This day is still salvageable, eh?"

Isaac followed Mr. Phillips upstairs to the foyer and then out the door. The older man walked with him to the street corner, pointed toward an alleyway behind the row of townhouses, and indicated the mews. He then stepped off the curb and headed toward the law office.

Isaac, holding the bottle of honey concoction in one hand, grasped the directions to Preece Farm in the other. He looked down at both, and a sense of relief washed over him. He had another chance—and this time, he was determined not to ruin it.

While the morning had been tumultuous for Isaac Tiffin, Mr. Bennet was having a grand time. As he always did, he held court over his breakfast table, tossing quips to his wife and daughter. Now, with the added pleasure of Mr. Blackwell's company, he had a third person to pepper with witticisms. Though Blackwell was not the quickest wit, he was the most effusive in his praise, and after a meal of kippers, eggs, toast, and compliments, Mr. Bennet was feeling ready to take on the world.

When the meal concluded, he clapped his hands together, rubbing them with enthusiasm. "Well, lady wife, Blackwell and I are off to tour the property. Do try not to miss us too terribly." He knew for certain his wife would not miss him in the slightest, as she had already made that clear.

Blackwell, ever the charmer, interjected, "Say not that you will not miss us, dearest madam, for it would crush our hearts to know you do not eagerly await our return." He swept a deep bow and kissed her hand.

Mrs. Bennet fluttered in response, as expected. "Oh, you," she said, blushing like a debutante.

Blackwell, undeterred by her feigned protestations, turned his attention to her daughter. "And you, mademoiselle, remember me fondly until this afternoon. Jusque-là, Cherie." His kiss upon her hand was received with far less warmth, a fact Mr. Bennet noted with quiet amusement.

It was at this moment that Bennet lost patience with the pageantry of Blackwell's affections. "Now, if you've finished making love to my wife and flustering my daughter, shall we go?"

Together, they made their way to the stable, where two horses awaited them. Bennet was not a great expert in horseflesh; he had only a few animals for work rather than for pleasure. Still, they were fit for the purpose of carrying their owner and his guest, allowing them to set off through the farmyard and toward the paddocks.

"The eastern side of the property holds the home farm fields," he called to Blackwell, who nodded enthusiastically. The boy seemed to do everything enthusiastically, which Bennet was pleased to see. "We can spy them beginning just there," he added, sweeping his arm wide to indicate rows of vegetables rolling away along the hills.

"Marvelous, marvelous," replied Blackwell. "Your gift for land management is only exceeded by your wisdom and wit, sir."

The compliment felt odd in Bennet's ears, but still, it was nice to be appreciated. He smiled, nodded, and turned his horse west. Past the tenant cottages were his pride and joy: the western cattle grazing land.

"This is really what I wanted to get your opinion on, Blackwell. What do you think of that?" He pulled up on a hill so they could look at the half dozen heads of fine Jersey cows dotting the landscape.

Blackwell observed, a serious expression on his face. "The land is beautiful, greener than I imagine even Ireland can boast. Are you planning to expand your pleasure gardens here, once you sell off the cattle?"

"Sell off the cattle?" Bennet sputtered, confused and more than a little irritated. "The cattle are the point, man."

Blackwell pulled up on the reins of his horse, readjusted his viewpoint now that he had more information, and tried again. "Of course, my apologies. It's just that your fields are so well-tended that I suddenly had the urge to hold picnics on their gentle slopes."

"Whyever would we want to cavort in the fields?" Mr. Bennet was beginning to wonder if this man might be as empty-headed as his flat-headed heir, Mr. Collins.

Blackwell tried to change the subject. "Is that the parcel of land you're attempting to buy?" He pointed beyond the hedgerow to where another set of paddocks ran parallel to those owned by Longbourn.

"Yes, but I received word the other day that the blasted deal had fallen through. I've half a mind to march over to the magistrate's house myself this very moment. Would you join me, boy? I might change Sir Lucas' mind about the purchase if he knew I kept such elegant company."

Blackwell's face clouded with something akin to genuine alarm. "The magistrate? Is that the Sir Lucas you speak of?"

"Yes, that he is, and a better friend to Longbourn cannot be found. I'm certain that if we talk this out, we can come to some sort of understanding. No time like the present. Let us go!"

"Ah," Blackwell said in growing desperation, trying to keep his host from hauling off to the magistrate's home. "If that's the same gentleman you speak of, I met him upon entering town. I told him I was heading to Longbourn, and he said the strangest thing to me. 'Longbourn, eh?' he said. 'Don't tell Bennet, but I'm quite proud of scuttling a little land deal over there. Need to keep that man in his place.' Do you know what he meant by that?" Blackwell watched for any reaction, and it didn't take long for his host to respond.

"Keep him in his place?! The nerve of the man! Well, he shall never again set foot on Longbourn property while I am alive, I can tell you that! Insufferable man, trying to keep me from expanding my domain. Is that not the mandate of the landed gentleman, to acquire more land?" Mr. Bennet fumed for quite some time, and Mr. Blackwell spent the rest of their outing happily soothing the elder man's spleen in a manner that did nothing but inflame it. By the time they returned to the house, Mr. Bennet was in such a great temper that he shut himself in his bookroom and refused to speak to anyone.

Mr. Blackwell, for his part, thought the morning had gone very well indeed.

Kitty heard the crash of the bookroom door and knew its meaning. Never had that portal been so abused, except when her father needed to vent his ire. Not wanting to be the focus of his anger, whatever its cause, she scurried to the front door, grabbed her bonnet and shawl, and opened it, only to find the front porch already occupied.

"Why, hello, Mr. Tiffin!" said Kitty, very much surprised to see him. "What a pleasant surprise to see you today. Would you like to come in?"

"No, I would not, thank you. I've been indoors far too long today as it is," barked Mr. Tiffin in his gruff manner, his blond brows drawn together in what she was coming to recognize as a frown of discomfort. "I came to give this to you," he handed her what looked like a bottle of vaguely green honey.

"Why, thank you, sir. We can always use more honey at the breakfast table," Kitty smiled, a little nonplussed but still grateful for the gift.

"It's not for the breakfast table; it's for you. It's a mixture for your summer asthma. You take a spoonful in the mornings, and it should help ease your sneezing. Grannie Tiffin swore by it for her complaint. I made it for you," this last came out in a smaller, more vulnerable tone that did something unfamiliar to Kitty's insides.

Kitty was shocked. Never had anyone thought so much of her comfort to go and make a mixture to improve her health. Not even the doctor, who did nothing more than feed his leeches. "I will treasure this gift and make sure I take the prescribed amount as you directed. I thank you most sincerely for thinking of me. Is there anything I can do for you in return?"

Mr. Tiffin looked exceedingly uncomfortable, shifting from one foot to the other. He seemed to be about to deny her request when he thought of something. "I am on an errand of business for Mr. Phillips," he said, pulling a piece of paper from his coat pocket. He unfolded it and read, "I am meant to visit, er, Preece Farm. Might you give me directions, if you know it? These seem to guide me only from the center of town, which I am no longer in."

From behind Kitty came the sound of Mr. Blackwell's silky tones and her mother's giggling response. If she stayed here for more than a moment, she would no doubt be forced into walking the garden with Mr. Blackwell, and she definitely did not want that privilege. Making a quick decision, Kitty nodded to herself and closed the front door behind her.

"I'll do you one better, Mr. Tiffin," Kitty said, knotting her bonnet under her chin. "I'll show you myself. Mr. Preece was one of my father's best tenants, so I know exactly where Preece Farm is. Let me guide you."

Mr. Tiffin blinked in surprise, but as Kitty was already stepping off the porch and climbing into his cart, any protestations appeared to be useless. "Very well," he grumbled, and, climbing into the box beside her, he set off down the road.

The drive through the Longbourn lands started quietly, save for Kitty's brief instructions along the way. Mr. Tiffin didn't seem to be the sort of person to start a conversation, so Kitty girded her loins, as it were, and dove in.

"What is it you like most about being a clerk?" She looked at her companion and watched his mercurial face darken more than she had ever seen it.

"I like nothing about being a clerk, since you ask," his reply was hard, as if chipped from granite. He tightened his hands on the reins so much that Kitty heard the leather creak.

Refusing to be deterred, she tried a different tack. "What's your favorite part of farming, then?"

Mr. Tiffin was silent for several moments, and Kitty felt her mind wandering off to try a new topic when he finally answered. "The way the land looks just as the sun rises. The fog on the hills wrapping the animals in a sort of blanket of clouds. Everything looks like you have the promise of only good things to come. The land always gives back more than you give it."

Kitty closed her eyes, imagined the fog-wrapped sheep, and smiled at the vision.

"Do you have anything you like as much as I like farming?" Mr. Tiffin asked, his voice coming from the darkness past her eyelids.

Kitty opened her eyes to see him looking down on her, his eyes softer than she had ever seen them.

Kitty tilted her head, thinking. "I liked my sister, I suppose. I adored her; I still do, but she got married and moved away a few years ago.

Everything was more fun with Lydia around, the days brighter and more exciting. She always had a way of turning even the most boring situations into a lark.

"I did everything I could to be like her, though she was younger than I. I still do, especially now that she's moved north. I never seem to get it quite right, though. I expect there is no one really like Lydia."

"You shouldn't try to be your sister. You'll always fail an impossible task like that."

Kitty laughed in surprise. "Are you always so bluntly truthful, Mr. Tiffin?"

Mr. Tiffin nodded as if it were the most natural thing in the world always to speak your mind so openly. "Grannie Tiffin raised me to believe that the truth is a precious seed that's planted in us by God when we're born. It's our job to nurture that gift, to water it and tend it, and take care of it. Some people leave the truth seed to wither and die, and then they lose hope in themselves. But if you protect the truth within you, if it survives the trials you face, one day it will bloom into a beautiful flower, and then you will be a true servant of God."

"That is beautiful," Kitty spoke in reverent tones. " I wish I could have met your grandmother. She sounds like a wonderful person. You said she raised you?"

"Aye, Grannie Tiffin was my only family for as long as I remember. There was an illness that swept through the village when I was younger, and it took my grandfather. My parents I lost...in an accident." His words trailed off into the wind that blew past the cart as they drove. A moment of silence filled the space between then, Mr. Tiffin staring ahead. Then, a minute later he continued. "After that it was just us two on the farm, working together. She's the only family I've had since. I 'spose I have no family at all now."

"No other siblings?" Kitty felt the strangeness of that idea keenly. She had lived all her life surrounded by siblings, until they all married and left. It was truly lonely without her sisters. Perhaps that was why she was speaking so openly with Mr. Tiffin, a near stranger. He was so easy to talk to.

"None."

"I could never imagine such a thing. Oh, turn here at the bent oak," Kitty said, giving directions before continuing. "I have four sisters—three older and one younger. Our house was always filled with noise, except on Sundays, of course," she smiled, thinking of the constant bustle that had been Longbourn during her childhood.

"That sounds horrifying. I couldn't stand to always be surrounded by people," Mr. Tiffin shuddered at the thought.

"It's not so bad as one might expect. There were plenty of arguments and tantrums, but there were also larks and adventures in abundance. There was always someone to share my secrets with. I liked that the most."

Around a bend in the hedged lane, they crested a hill. Below them stretched a tidy little farm, surrounded by spring wheat fields. Mr. Tiffin pulled the cart to a stop beneath the branches of a sprawling oak.

Kitty pointed to a neat farm in the vale below. "That's Preece Farm there. It looks as if Mr. Preece the Elder is in the farmyard. Was it he you needed to speak to?"

"Yes, I suppose. Let's get this over with," grumbled Mr. Tiffin, returning to his usual surly disposition. Kitty hadn't noticed how open and relaxed he had seemed during the drive over, talking about his home life and his grandmother. She regretted the shift in his demeanor and found herself unexpectedly disappointed by it.

Mr. Tiffin navigated the cart down the lane and into the Preece Farm yard, where Mr. Preece was approaching.

"Mr. Preece?" Mr. Tiffin inquired, bringing the cart to a stop.

"Good afternoon, Mr. Preece," Kitty said politely. "I hope you are well."

Mr. Preece said nothing, merely nodding. His face was as unreadable as a block of wood. Kitty didn't remember much about the Preece family, but she had spoken to them at the church reception following the passing of Mr. Preece's father. They had been naturally despondent then, but she didn't recall them being so guarded. Perhaps it was because she came with a stranger?

Mr. Tiffin stepped down from the driving box and approached with his hand outstretched. "I am Isaac Tiffin, working for Mr. Phillips, the attorney."

At the mention of Mr. Phillips, Mr. Preece became even more stoic, if that were possible.

"I have come because Mr. Phillips does not have a copy of your father's second will. Would you mind if I took the original for duplication? I have orders to copy it and return it as soon as possible."

"There is no second will. Father wrote one up when we were lads, and that's been with the lawyer for years."

Mr. Tiffin adjusted the brim of his hat, standing to his full and imposing height. "I am new with the law practice, so I don't know the particulars. I only know that Mr. Phillips sent me here to pick up a document he says your father told him would be here. Is he wrong?"

Mr. Preece seemed to notice the shift in Mr. Tiffin's demeanor and became even more defensive. His shoulders stiffened, and his eyes darted toward the house as though searching for an escape route.

"Of course he's wrong. I'm the eldest, so my father left the farm to me. That's what father's will said, and you can tell Mr. Phillips that if he's lost it, that's his problem, not mine. Now if you'll excuse me, I have work to do." Mr. Preece turned abruptly and strode toward the house, slamming the door loudly behind him.

Mr. Tiffin stared at the closed door for a long moment before returning to the cart. He climbed back up beside Kitty and grasped the reins in clenched fists. His jaw was set so firmly that Kitty half expected to hear his teeth crack as he snapped the reins and drove off.

Kitty sat in silence, trying to process what had just happened. She had expected Mr. Tiffin to be the sort of man who would stand his ground, given how forthright he had been with her so far. But now, they were leaving without a word of protest. Did the man who always spoke his mind simply run out of things to say? And why did that thought bother her so much?

Isaac wouldn't admit it to himself, but he had panicked. Having Miss Bennet there—an audience whose esteem seemed to matter more to him than he cared to acknowledge—had caused his mind to go blank. The moment Mr. Preece denied the existence of the very document Isaac had come to retrieve, he froze.

If he had been alone, he might have had the presence of mind to respond in his usual forthright manner. But feeling her gaze on him, the young lady who had so kindly offered a newcomer her assistance, embarrassed him more than he cared to admit. And so, like a buck staring down the barrel of a rifle, he was unable to come up with a single response.

Isaac berated himself as he retraced his route back to Longbourn. It was obvious to him that something was amiss. He could, of course, take things at face value and assume the farmer's son was telling the truth. But that would cast doubt on Mr. Phillips' credibility, and Isaac rather suspected his employer was too astute to make such a mistake, especially regarding the existence of a second will.

"Do you know Mr. Phillips well?" Isaac asked, chewing on the edge of a thought like a stalk of wheat. He had met Miss Bennet in the Phillips' garden, but that didn't necessarily mean they were closely acquainted.

"Intimately," she replied, as if countering his very thoughts. "He is my uncle."

"And your uncle—would you say he is known as an honest man with a good memory?" Isaac pressed, wanting to confirm his assumptions before acting on them.

Miss Bennet smiled fondly. "My uncle is the very best of men. Surely you've gathered that in your own dealings with him?"

"I have, but the picture Mr. Preece paints of him is in an entirely different style. I needed to be certain I wasn't being misled by my new employer." If Mr. Phillips was indeed the competent lawyer he appeared to be, then any error, if it existed, must lie with Mr. Preece.

Isaac rubbed his chin thoughtfully, his mind turning over the problem. "Why would Mr. Preece deny the existence of a second will when Mr. Phillips claims to have heard of it directly from his father?"

"Perhaps he lost it himself?" Miss Bennet suggested. "I know when my sister misplaced something, she would often blame one of us to shift the attention away from herself."

"Shift the attention..." Isaac mused, considering the idea. Perhaps Mr. Preece was trying to shift the blame to Mr. Phillips, but why? "Aren't there two Preece brothers?"

Kitty nodded. "Mr. Preece, known as Young Dave, and Mr. Norman Preece, who is, in fact, the younger brother."

"We know there's a second will, and the elder Preece brother insists it doesn't exist. Either he's wrong, or he's lying. I need to figure out which." Isaac's thoughts began to align into a plan. "It seems I need to speak with the second brother. Perhaps he will be more accommodating."

Miss Bennet laughed. "I don't think things would go particularly well if you approached them both at once. Perhaps it's best to find a time to speak with Norman Preece alone?"

"Indeed," Isaac nodded, tugging at the brim of his hat. "This is going to require strategy, and I'm not the best strategist."

"No," agreed Miss Bennet, surprising him. Isaac looked over to find her smiling with mischief in her blue eyes. "But there is one thing you're good at that might be more useful than any strategy." She paused, watching him closely, as if waiting for him to bite.

Isaac waited for her to continue, and when it became clear she was expecting a response, he asked, "And that is? Blurting out the truth at the least opportune moments?"

Miss Bennet shook her head, smiling. "Farming."

For the rest of the journey, the little cart bounced along as they planned. By the time Isaac turned the cart onto the drive in front of Longbourn House, he had a clear idea of what he was going to do—thanks, in large part, to his lovely companion.

He felt prepared and calm, a state that was unusual for him. Having someone to talk things through with was infinitely better than muttering to himself while plowing the fields, his usual way of handling problems. Moreover, Miss Bennet had a fresh perspective on the people at Longbourn, one that came from years of observing the behavior of others. Whether this insight stemmed from being raised among so many sisters, Isaac wasn't certain. But he was sure of one thing—he wanted to know more about her.

Unfortunately, that understanding would have to wait. As he slowed the cart, Isaac noticed a man standing on the Longbourn porch. He wore a well-cut suit, at least to Isaac's untrained eye, and with his darkly handsome looks, he seemed to be glowering down his nose at the pair of them.

Ignoring the tall stranger, Isaac jumped down from the cart and came around to assist Miss Bennet. "Thank you for your assistance, Miss Bennet," he said, taking her hand and pressing a gentlemanly kiss to it. "I'll take your counsel under advisement as I plan my next moves."

He reached into the box behind the seat and retrieved the bottle he had brought for her. "And don't forget your treatment," he added with a warm smile.

Returning to the driver's side of the cart, Isaac vaulted back onto the seat and flicked the reins to urge Mabel forward. As the cart trundled toward Meryton proper, he felt a grin tugging at his lips. He could sense the tall stranger's eyes boring into his back, the frustration and jealousy almost tangible.

That, for some reason, pleased Isaac more than he cared to admit. It seemed the day hadn't been a complete waste after all.

Kitty Bennet stood on the drive in front of Longbourn, her gaze fixed on Mr. Blackwell, who glared toward Isaac Tiffin. The contrast between the two men was striking. One was a farmer at heart, light-haired and light on charm. The other was dark, brooding, and sleek—like a shark, or perhaps a panther.

As a child, Kitty had spent countless secret hours dreaming of the man who would swoop into Meryton and choose her above all her sisters. Unfortunately, she could never imagine a face for him, nor could she believe that anyone would choose her over Lydia.

Now, here was Mr. Blackwell, frowning down from on high, clearly angry that she was spending time with another man. It took all of Kitty's willpower not to laugh at the absurdity of it.

"Miss Bennet, who was that man?" Mr. Blackwell descended the front steps and loomed over her. Kitty bristled, not appreciating his imposing posture.

"Mr. Tiffin? He's my uncle's new clerk at the attorney's office." Kitty took a step toward the house, but Mr. Blackwell moved to block her path.

"I don't think it's proper for a young lady to travel about with a single man alone." Mr. Blackwell grasped her arm with his slender fingers. The grip was cold and unyielding, reminding her of the image of a shark—menacing and calculating, matching the dangerous look in his eyes.

"I can see your point," Kitty replied, her voice steady despite the unease creeping up her spine. "I shall endeavor to assist my family in a manner that appears more proper in the future. Now, if you'll excuse me, I need to speak with my mother." She attempted to break free of his hold, but his grip tightened, stubborn as steel.

"But you forgot," Mr. Blackwell said, his voice smooth, "you promised to show me the lovely gardens here at Longbourn." Finally, a smile stretched across his face—a toothy grin that did nothing to diminish his resemblance to the king of the sea.

"And yet," Kitty countered, her gaze hardening, "you yourself said it would not be proper to spend time alone with a single man. So, I'm afraid I must pass that privilege to someone more suitable. My father, perhaps?"

"Is this because of that man in the cart?" Mr. Blackwell's expression darkened, and his smile faltered, replaced by a flash of something darker. "Were you out having a tryst with him?" His smile vanished completely, but his teeth still gleamed, more like the snarl of an animal than a man.

Kitty's discomfort grew with every passing second. She wished, more than anything, that Mr. Tiffin were there—someone brash and loud enough to disrupt the situation with his overlarge presence. In all the time she had sat beside him in that cart, never once had she felt threatened by his size or manner. But Mr. Blackwell was a different matter entirely, his demeanor growing more menacing by the second.

"Please let me go, Mr. Blackwell," she said, her voice trembling despite her best efforts. "I wish to return to the house. Your accusations are uncalled for, and I do not wish to speak with you anymore."

"Oh, you don't need to speak," Mr. Blackwell growled in a low, menacing tone, his grip tightening on her arm. "But you will listen to what I have to say." Without another word, he began to walk toward the side of the house, pulling her along with him. Kitty had no choice but to follow, her only other option being to be dragged.

Mr. Blackwell stalked into the cutting garden, only stopping once he was out of sight of the drawing room windows. "Now you listen here," he said, his voice low and threatening. "I've come a very long way to see you, and you've done nothing to show the slightest gratitude for the effort. So now, you're going to change your behavior, or I'll make things uncomfortable for you."

Two warring emotions rose within Kitty in response to Mr. Blackwell's demand: fear and rebellion. For a long moment, the fear threatened to overwhelm her, but in the end, it was rebellion that won out. "I never asked you to come here, and it is certainly not my intention to change my behavior. I did not seek your interest, sir. Kindly leave me be."

"I have no interest in you, you dowdy chit," Mr. Blackwell spat, the foulness of his words stinging her skin as he leaned down until his nose was mere inches from hers. "It's your dowry I need. And because I need it, I will not be leaving here until I have that money. So unless you want to see your parents trapped in a fire some night, I suggest you become the model of a smitten young lady very quickly."

Panic surged through Kitty's veins, and her stomach churned violently. He had threatened her family. The realization hit her like a physical blow—this was all her fault. The only reason Mr. Blackwell had come here was because of the lie she had told in her letter to Lydia. That blasted letter! If only Kitty had been content with her small, insignificant life, satisfied to be the forgotten spinster among the famous Bennet sisters, none of this would have happened. But here she was, trapped in the grip of a money-crazed madman, powerless to escape.

Unless...

"I cannot marry you. I am already engaged to Mr. Tiffin."

CHAPTER THREE

T he shock on Mr. Blackwell's face reverberated through his body, loosening his grip just enough for Kitty to break free. She didn't hesitate—skittering quickly toward the kitchen door, she slipped inside the house in moments. Making her way toward the sanctuary of her bedroom, Kitty didn't slow down until several doors stood between her and Mr. Blackwell's furious anger.

Pressing her back against the closed bedroom door, Kitty exhaled a shaky breath, her pulse still racing. Her mind buzzed with the shocking revelation: Mr. Blackwell had known about her fake dowry and had come to Longbourn with the express purpose of marrying her. Marrying her—the invisible Bennet sister. The absurdity of it struck her like a punch to the gut.

She crossed the room and approached the window, leaning her shoulder against the molding. Her hands slid into her pockets as she allowed herself a moment to relax. That was, until she felt the very familiar weight of a letter resting against the fabric. She hadn't finished reading Lydia's letter yet, and now, her suspicion grew that it contained information of far greater importance than she had first realized.

Sitting down on her bed, Kitty carefully withdrew the letter and held it up to the candlelight. The flickering flame illuminated Lydia's untidy handwriting, and Kitty quickly scanned through the words, searching for the spot where she had stopped reading. There it was—halfway down the page.

In any case, before I go on I simply must tell you about a visit we had from Wickham's cousin not long after I received your letter. Blackwell, and he's the most charming man—next to my Wickham, of course, who is the best of men—that I have ever encountered. He came to visit us after suffering a bad turn at the gaming tables—you know how men are.

Well, it wasn't long after Blackwell's arrival that the subject of your dowry came up at dinner. I don't precisely recall how it happened, but suddenly we were discussing you, Kitty—if you can believe it. Blackwell became quite fascinated when he heard of your great fortune. My sister, the heiress! He wanted to know everything about you: whether you were courting anyone, if you were planning to visit a proper city to seek suitors, that sort of thing. La! It was nothing but question after question for days. I'll admit, I grew bored of it all very quickly—what woman wants to be interrogated about her sister?

I told Blackwell so. I said, "If you're so curious about my sister, why not ask her yourself?" I thought he would smarten up and return to paying the proper attention to me, as he had been doing—so gallant! But then, quick as lightning, he replied, "Too true, madam, I shall away to visit this Kitty of yours and see if I can get the answers to my questions directly."

So, he's on his way to you, Kitty—the second most handsome man in all of creation, coming to visit my sister! Isn't that just the most delightful thing? I'm positively certain you're about to have the most wonderful time. And when the engagement happens, do be sure to make me your matron of honor, of course.

Write to me soon—I simply must be the very first person to hear all about it.

Kisses!

Lydia

And so, it was all laid bare: Blackwell had heard about the dowry from Lydia, and had taken it into his head that the money would be his. But of course, the dowry did not exist, and even if it had, she could never marry a man so mercenary. She, the last Bennet sister, was meant to care for her parents in their old age. How could she abandon that responsibility to align herself with a man who cared only for money? The thought made her blood run cold.

If only Lydia had not gossiped to Wickham and his cousin. It was true that Kitty shouldn't have lied in the first place. Had she kept her daydreams to herself, they never would have spiraled out of control like this. What a tangled mess she had landed herself in!

Leaning back, Kitty dropped Lydia's letter onto the counterpane. What was she to do? If only Lydia were here to talk to, or one of her older sisters. Though they all already thought her quite foolish, and this situation would only confirm it. Well, she didn't have a sister to turn to, but she did have what Lydia had left behind, and perhaps that would be enough.

Getting up, Kitty rummaged through her trunk, pulling out an old dress Lydia had once given her. It was far too long, but Kitty didn't mind. She also retrieved a ribbon that Lydia had discarded, as well as a broken fan from a drawer—the one Lydia had carelessly tossed aside after an evening at the assemblies.

Kitty arranged the items on a chair, laying them out as if a woman had worn them and then simply vanished before her eyes.

"Now, Lydia, what should I do?" Kitty muttered, her fingers trailing over the dress. "I've lied to you, it's true. But now I've also lied to Mr. Blackwell, about an engagement that never took place. If I tell him the truth, he will be furious, and I know he'll demand that I marry him. That cannot happen. But Mr. Tiffin never lies, so how could he go along with such a scheme?"

Kitty sighed, feeling unsatisfied with her silent confidant. Lydia, of course, offered no responses. It was much easier to talk to Mr. Tiffin. He had genuinely listened to her, had seemed to care about her words. Had he not promised to follow her advice? No one had ever done that before. At home, she was always told to keep quiet.

Kitty's gaze landed on the bottle of medicine Mr. Tiffin had prepared for her. He was so thoughtful. Perhaps he would know what to do about this tangled situation. Yes, she would seek his counsel, if only to ask for his help in keeping Mr. Blackwell's interest at bay.

With a plan forming in her mind, Kitty nodded to herself and took a sip of the green honey. It tasted sweet and grassy, with the faint warmth of memories. It tasted of the day she had lost a letter but found a friend.

That evening, dinner at the Phillips' townhouse was more than a little awkward. Isaac kept replaying the events of the day in his mind. It had been filled with so many highs and lows that it left his head spinning. He couldn't decide how to categorize it—confusing, frustrating, and strangely exhilarating all at once. After the dishes had been cleared away and Mrs. Phillips had retired, leaving the men to their port, it was time for Isaac to catch Mr. Phillips up on the day's events since they'd parted that morning.

"Sir, I thank you again for the opportunity to continue working for you. I know next to nothing about the law, and I've only been inside an office three times in my entire life. What happened today was proof of my ignorance."

"Come now, my boy," Mr. Phillips said with a reassuring smile, "No filly starts a race on a new track running full tilt."

Isaac chuckled softly. "I rather see myself as more of a draft horse than a thoroughbred, sir," he said, allowing himself a small smile. At least they were talking about something he understood.

"One does get quite a crick in their neck standing next to you," Mr. Phillips said, a light chuckle escaping him as he acknowledged Isaac's size without mocking it.

Isaac appreciated the rare moments when someone accepted him at face value. It made him feel seen, not just for his height, but for who he was as a person.

"So," Mr. Phillips continued, leaning back in his chair and taking a sip of his port, "How did things go at the Preece farm?"

Isaac fidgeted with his untouched glass. "Not as well as I had hoped. I met the elder Mr. Preece, and he insisted there was no second will to give me."

Mr. Phillips, whose face almost always carried a smile, sobered at once and sat up straight. "Unfortunately for us, that is not the case. I was hired by the elder Mr. Preece to draft a will that would ensure Young Dave inherited the farm, but something changed in the last year."

He paused, his eyes hardening as he recalled the details. "When Farmer Preece took ill, he wrote a second will and instructed me to destroy the first. That second will should have been delivered to me after the man died, but it never made it off the farm. Now, with Young Dave insisting it doesn't exist, I need to know what happened to it. Are you up to the challenge, Tiffin?"

Isaac squared his shoulders, his resolve firming. "It matters very much to me that I see this through, Mr. Phillips. I intend to return to Preece Farm tomorrow to speak with Mr. Norman Preece. Perhaps he knows what happened to the second will."

Mr. Phillips regarded him with an approving nod. "Good, because I won't trust the word of a man who lies to my employees, that's for certain. Let me know what you find, and be careful. Something strange is happening up there."

"Aye, sir. I will," Isaac replied, his voice steady but his mind already racing ahead to what awaited him at Preece Farm.

Isaac was up before dawn the next day. He took a cup of tea with a heel of bread and some cheese at the staff table, trying to blend into the background as the household staff went about their business. When he finished, he left the house and made his way straight to the stables. In minutes, he had Mabel hitched to her cart, and together they set off on a journey that felt oddly solitary, now that he was alone this time.

Not one to lose his way once he'd traveled a road before, Isaac made good time, only needing to pull over once to let a farmer pass with a flock of sheep. He did, however, find himself pausing at the top of the hill above Preece Farm. His thoughts drifted to a certain bright-eyed young lady who had accompanied him the last time he was here. She had surprised him with her openness, talking about what it was like to be the last unmarried sister in a family of women. It seemed such a different life from his, isolated as he was in the Cumbrian hills. Somehow, he got the sense that she was lonelier than he had ever been.

Shaking his head to clear it of thoughts of Miss Bennet, Isaac guided Mabel down the lane and into the farmyard of Preece Farm, bracing himself for what felt like a battle ahead. His shoulders were tense as he brought the cart to a halt, half expecting Young Dave to leap out of a doorway and run him off the property. It wouldn't have been the first time Isaac encountered hostility upon an unannounced visit, and he doubted it would be the last.

Instead, a tall, leaner version of the elder Mr. Preece emerged from the barn, a coil of rope slung over one shoulder. He paused when he spotted Isaac, assessing him with a quick glance before giving a curt nod and stepping forward.

"Morning, sir. Welcome to Preece Farm. What brings you here?"

Isaac straightened, recalling Miss Bennet's advice to lean into his farming background. It was sound counsel, and he resolved to make good use of it.

"Good morning," he said, doffing his cap. "I'm Isaac Tiffin, recently settled in Meryton. I'm working under Mr. Phillips, who I understand assisted your father with some legal matters. Truth be told, I'm new to clerking—a sheep farmer born and bred. And, well..." He let out a small chuckle, glancing around the yard. "I miss the land. Was wondering if you might need an extra set of hands for the day? I'd be that glad to lend my strength to the work."

"Volunteering to grunt around the farm?" A broad grin spread across Mr. Preece's long, weathered face. "How can I say no? Tiffin, you said? Well, I'm Norman Preece, and I'd be more than pleased to have the help. Truth be told, it's just me most days." He extended a hand.

Isaac took it, his brow furrowing slightly. "Alone most days? Do you not have an older brother, Mr. Preece?"

"Norman, please. There are too many 'Mr. Preeces' around this place, and I've never stood much on ceremony. By the time we've mucked out a stall or two together, you won't either. Come on, let's start with the girls—I can hear them hollering already."

Norman strode toward the barn, and Isaac followed, stepping into the earthy, warm air of the space. Inside, three placid milk cows, the "girls," he assumed, were tied to a rail.

Isaac didn't need instruction. Rolling up his sleeves, he fell naturally into the rhythm of milking, his large hands steady on the task. The familiar scents of hay and warm animals filled the barn, grounding him. With each pull, the sound of milk hitting the pail was almost meditative. Isaac leaned his cheek against the cow's flank, its heat seeping into his skin, a soothing reminder of his old life.

After tending to the girls, it was time to wrangle the bull back into the paddock so Norman could let the cows graze for the day. Norman was a skilled farmer, capable of handling the massive Jersey bull on his own, but with Isaac's strength at hand, they bypassed his usual routine of chasing the bull into a corner. Isaac's brawn made it easy for him to grab the bull's horns and deftly wrap them with a rope.

"That's some fine work, Tiffin," Norman said, slapping him on the back as they led the bull to his paddock. "It's clear you've done this sort of work before."

"All my life," Isaac replied with a grin. "And please, call me Isaac."

"What brought you to the attorney's employ, then? Not often you see a farmer change careers."

Isaac hesitated, a flicker of something passing through his eyes before he answered. "It was my Grannie Tiffin's last wish. Though she married a Cumbrian, she was originally from Meryton and wanted me to live here after she passed. She asked her attorney to look after me, and he took me in."

"I'm sorry you lost your Nan," Norman said, his voice quiet for a moment. "It was the hardest thing I've ever done—watching my father take his last breath. I miss him more than I can say."

Norman doffed his hat, his eyes downcast for a moment, lost in memory.

"I cannot imagine how hard that was for your family," Isaac said quietly, genuinely feeling the weight of the words.

"Thank ye kindly, Tiffin," Norman responded. "Now, are you up for some fence mending, or have I worked you ragged already?"

"We're just getting warmed up," Isaac replied with a smile.

Norman led him across the farm, and together they repaired half a dozen spots where the stone fences had crumbled. The property was truly beautiful, well cared for. It was the sort of place Isaac would want for his own one day... if he couldn't get his own farm back, that is.

By noon, they circled back to the farmhouse, and Norman offered Isaac lunch. Isaac hesitated, aware that the elder Mr. Preece might be around, and politely declined.

"Is there any way to thank you for all your help, then?" Norman asked. "If I can't feed you, there has to be something you need. Fresh cheese?"

"I'll gladly take some cheese," Isaac said. "The cook at Phillips' house would be most grateful. But I'd also like to ask a question, if you don't mind."

"Ask anything. I'll answer if I can," Norman replied, leaning against the kitchen door and crossing his legs at the ankles. He wiped his brow with a scrap of cloth, his expression open.

"Do you happen to know where your father's second will might be? Mr. Phillips sent me to borrow it for copying." Isaac waited, barely breathing, to gauge Norman's reaction.

"A second will?" Norman frowned, his expression sharpening. "My father never mentioned it to me, but..." He trailed off, glancing back toward the house. Straightening, he lowered his voice to a near whisper. "I do remember Pa arguing with Young Dave about something before he died. The word 'will' came up, but I can't say for sure. I'm sorry I'm not more help."

"Thank you anyway," Isaac said warmly. "For the lovely morning doing what I love, and for letting me spend time on your beautiful farm. It's quite a spot you've got here. Cherish it."

"I'm glad someone appreciates it," Norman replied with a faint smile. "I just wish my brother felt the same way."

"Not a lover of the farmer's life, eh?" Isaac asked, his tone light but probing, sensing there might be more to uncover.

Norman hesitated, then sighed. "Not since we went to visit our uncle on the coast as boys. The moment Young Dave saw the ships, he was hooked. Loved nothing but the sea ever since."

Half a wheel of cheese in hand, Isaac bade his goodbyes to Norman Preece, turned Mabel toward home, and spent the rest of the journey to Meryton chewing over his thoughts.

So, a man who dreams of setting sail is trapped on land? That's enough to curdle anyone's blood. Isaac knew the feeling all too well—the longing to be elsewhere, bound by duty to a life you never chose.

As the miles passed, Isaac began to form a theory about what was happening at Preece Farm—and he didn't like it one bit.

Kitty awoke to find the household in chaos. John, the harried footman, passed her as she left her bedroom, struggling with an unfamiliar clothes chest. In the foyer, Griffiths, the butler, had called a stable boy over, and as Kitty passed them on her way to the dining room, she overheard instructions for a carriage to be brought around. Then, seated at her usual breakfast table—Lydia's usual breakfast, rather—Kitty heard her mother's wailing from upstairs, loud enough to rattle the china. Something was most certainly wrong.

She noted with some satisfaction that Mr. Blackwell was absent from his usual seat, where Jane once sat, allowing Kitty to enjoy her meal in peace—well, relative peace, considering the chaos unfolding in her mother's boudoir.

Kitty ate quickly, as any lady was permitted, drank a second fortifying cup of tea, and then made her way upstairs to the lion's den to uncover the truth. In her mother's chambers, both the housekeeper and the lady's maid, Dunsmore, were attempting to console the grief-stricken Mrs. Bennet, who lay upon her bed.

"Mama, whatever is the matter?" Kitty asked, not the least bit alarmed. Her mother's frequent nerve attacks were as much a part of life as spring rains or Kitty's own sneezes. England was wet, Kitty was sneezy, and Mrs. Bennet was volatile. Such was the natural order of things.

"You! It must be your fault! Thankless girl!" Mrs. Bennet wailed, flinging herself dramatically onto the bed. "I have done nothing but slave away for your comfort, day in and day out, working my fingers to the bone, and this is how you repay me?"

"I am certain you are correct, Mama," Kitty replied with practiced patience. "What is it that I am at fault for this time?" She kept her tone as gentle as possible—sometimes that was enough to defuse her mother's nervous energy.

Not today.

"You drove him away! The most charming, the most handsome, the most elegant man in the kingdom, and you sent him packing! Now you are doomed to spinsterhood, Kitty—doomed!" Mrs. Bennet dissolved into tears, sobbing dramatically into her lace-edged hand-kerchief.

Now Kitty understood. Her fabricated story had sent Mr. Black-well away from Longbourn—exactly as she had intended. But the success of her plan had come at the cost of dashing her mother's hopes for her marriage prospects. Kitty's relief was tinged with guilt, though she wasn't quite sure why.

"My poor nerves! I cannot take this betrayal, Kitty, I simply cannot! I almost had all of you wed, and before Mrs. Lucas had even married off Mariah! And now I will be a laughingstock, the joke of the county! They'll look at me when I pass and snicker. 'There goes the Bennet woman. Her daughter was going to marry Mr. Blackwell, but couldn't bring him up to scratch.' Oh, how could you?" The crying began anew.

Guilt twisted in Kitty's heart, and she immediately wished she had handled things differently. Marriage was such a tricky business, and she knew that most women never truly loved their husbands. Yes, Mr. Blackwell was a rogue—high-handed and mercenary—but weren't most men like that? Take Wickham, for instance, who had chased after one of her sisters only to run off with another.

Perhaps that was the only sort of man Kitty could ever attract. And now, as her mother had so dramatically stated, she had ruined it. "I'm sorry, Mama," she murmured, feeling genuine regret.

"Whatever did you say to drive Blackwell off? He was so taken with you, I thought for sure he would propose..." Mrs. Bennet sniffled through her sobs.

Kitty felt a jolt of panic. How could she explain their conversation without revealing her fabricated dowry story? After a brief pause, she said, "I had just returned from helping Mr. Tiffin meet with a Longbourn tenant when Mr. Blackwell saw us. He seemed to believe

Mr. Tiffin and I were... involved in something untoward, which wasn't the case at all, Mama. You must believe me."

"Who is this Mr. Tiffin you speak of? Why have I never heard of him?"

"He's Uncle Phillips' new law clerk. He only arrived in Meryton a few days ago." Kitty shifted slightly. "Anyway, I had driven out with Mr. Tiffin to Preece Farm—you know, Mr. Preece the Elder passed away just a few days ago. Mr. Tiffin, being from Cumbria, needed directions, so I helped him find his way. In the spirit of neighborly generosity, as you taught me."

Kitty could feel herself rambling, but since she was already in the middle of the tale, she figured she might as well finish it. To her surprise, it was going unexpectedly well. She had danced around her lie to Lydia quite neatly.

"But when we returned, Mr. Blackwell saw us, as I said, and he became furious and threw a tantrum. He was terribly rude, saying the most uncouth things about Mr. Tiffin and me. I simply couldn't tolerate it. I told him he needn't bother proposing because I was already engaged, and then I turned and left him speechless."

"Already engaged?!" Mrs. Bennet sat up suddenly from the pillows supporting her as she reclined on the bed. "Do not tell me you've been secretly engaged this whole time!"

"No, that's not what I meant," Kitty's panic returned as she realized her mother was misunderstanding her explanation. "I simply told Mr. Blackwell..." But she didn't have a chance to finish.

"So, you've just gotten engaged?" Mrs. Bennet interrupted, her eyes brightening. "Is it to this Mr. Tiffin fellow?" She clasped Kitty's hands, her tear-streaked face lighting up with a wide grin. "Why, of course! You cheeky girl, stringing one man along while secretly engaged to another! I should have known you were as clever as Lydia. She always knew how to make the officers dangle after her. No wonder Mr. Blackwell was so angry—he'd lost the battle!"

Mrs. Bennet leapt out of the bed, forgetting her previous infirmity. "My darling Kitty, engaged!" She giggled and patted Kitty's cheek before rushing from the room, calling for her husband.

Kitty stood frozen in the bedroom, her hands clasped before her as if in prayer. She needed divine intervention to get out of this latest scrape. What was she to do now?

Isaac returned to Meryton an hour after noon, in good spirits. Now that he had actionable information to share with Mr. Phillips, he felt a sense of purpose. Plus, he had spent the morning doing what he loved—farming. It was a shame his Grannie Tiffin had wanted a better life for him. Farming had been the best life imaginable. But now, it was the sort of life that was considered "beneath" him. He had been elevated to the business class, plucked from his beloved Cumbria, and forced to navigate a world that felt as if he were blindfolded in a dark room.

Ah well, the expectations of loved ones had to be respected. Isaac would make his way in the world as his Grannie Tiffin had wanted. Still, there had been something so satisfying about working the land, out in the sunshine, with a mortar pail in his hand, lifting stones alongside Norman Preece.

Now there was a man who truly loved his work. Isaac envied him that—his passion for the farm was clear—but not his troubles. That was certain. As Isaac turned the final corner, aiming Mabel's cart to-

ward the stable, he chewed his lip thoughtfully. Spending the morning
with Norman had revealed two things: One, Norman loved that farm
with all his heart. And two, his brother was lying about the second will.
The argument Norman mentioned might also have been fabricated,
but Isaac was sure of one thing—Norman was used to working the
land by himself. His brother, however, didn't want to be a farmer. His
clean shoes told that story clearly.

A farmer's boots were always muddy because his fields were always
muddy. Isaac's own boots were caked in dirt after a morning of tramp-
ing around Preece Farm. But when he met the elder Preece brother,
his boots were as neat as a pin—a clear sign that he wasn't working
the land he supposedly loved. He wanted the farm, that much was
obvious, but what for? If he didn't care about the soil, if he craved a
bigger life... did that mean he only wanted the farm to sell it?

The thought sent a chill down Isaac's spine. How could a man
sell the farm out from under his brother, especially when the brother
loved it so? It was all conjecture for now, so Isaac would wait for
further discussion with his employer before drawing any conclusions.
But something was definitely off, and it left him feeling uneasy.

The unease only deepened when he spotted a familiar figure waiting in the shadows beside the stable. *I must be imagining things,* he
thought, shaking off the vision of a cloaked Miss Bennet standing
beneath the eaves. He drove the cart into the stableyard, thanked the
stable hands, and then turned back toward the spot where he had seen
her. What if she was really there? Isaac laughed at the absurdity of
it—Miss Bennet waiting to speak with him. With only a moment's
hesitation, he shoved his hands in his pockets and headed down the
street toward the attorney's office.

And suddenly, despite the absurdity of it, there she was. Miss Bennet stood in a navy cloak that melted into the shadows, her chestnut

hair tucked neatly under a straw bonnet. She turned to face him, her expression full of nervous anticipation, and when she caught his eye, her face broke into a smile. She stepped into the sunlight, and Isaac's heart skipped a beat. He missed a step, caught himself, then hesitantly continued toward her.

"Miss Bennet, I see you are well," Isaac said, his voice tight. He cleared his throat, feeling a sudden dryness in his mouth. Perhaps he was simply thirsty from his morning's work.

"Hello, Mr. Tiffin! I'm so glad to see you." She paused, glancing around, her voice dropping to a whisper. "I have something I need to speak with you about, but I'd rather not be seen talking to you by my family. Might we take a walk to the churchyard?"

Not want to be seen speaking with him? The warmth that had blossomed in Isaac's chest began to fade. Of course, she didn't want to be seen with him—what young lady would? He was a giant of a man, more bear than human, always saying the wrong thing at the wrong time. Years of mockery in Cumbria had hardened him to such things. He had learned to keep his distance from the village, spending most of his time working the farm. He was unused to company, unused to being noticed, and even less accustomed to having a lady seek his attention.

His eyes dropped to the cobblestones beneath his feet. "Lead on, if you please." Isaac swept a hand before him, his tone muted.

"Wonderful," Miss Bennet replied, stepping briskly down the street. She glanced over her shoulder toward the law office before crossing to the far side of the road, heading toward the church spire that stood as Meryton's most prominent landmark. Isaac followed, careful to keep a few paces behind her. Occasionally, Miss Bennet would glance back to make sure he was still trailing her.

When they passed through the iron gate into the churchyard, she stopped, sighed, and turned to face him.

"Now then," Miss Bennet began, her heart-shaped face lifting toward him, her eyes wide with concern. "Thank you for agreeing to speak with me. I'm afraid I've thrown us into a rather large pickle, and I'm desperate for your advice on how we can get out of it."

"Thrown 'us' into a pickle, miss?" Isaac furrowed his brow, confusion etching his features. "Forgive me, but I do not understand. I'm most willing to help you, but I'd need you to explain before I can offer any assistance."

Miss Bennet closed her eyes, took a deep breath, and then covered her face with gloved hands. Her voice, muffled by the leather, trembled slightly. "I may have... intimated to my mother that we are affianced."

This stopped Isaac dead in his tracks. "Engaged? You and I? Do they not see how absurd that is? I'm a jumped-up farmer, and you're a gentleman's daughter. It's... it's patently ridiculous that I would... that you would..." His words faltered, and he took several churning steps away, his thoughts spiraling out of control.

"Ridiculous," he finished weakly, his voice trailing off, unable to say the truth aloud.

"Yes, I can see how you might think that," Miss Bennet said, her voice gentle, but there was a faint, wry smile tugging at the corner of her lips. "But the Bennets are a very liberal family when it comes to matters of marriage. My youngest sister was the first of us to marry, and under... rather eccentric circumstances."

Isaac stared at her, the words swirling in his mind, but he couldn't seem to find a way to make sense of them. Dressed in her neat little cloak and bonnet, she looked every inch the lady she was — poised, composed, and elegant. He, on the other hand, was a filthy mess, caked in mud with his boots covered in the same grime that had marked his hands and skin for years. There was no universe where the two of them could ever belong together. The thought of a connection between them left Isaac feeling light-headed, as if the ground beneath him had suddenly shifted.

He took a steadying breath, unwilling to explore that feeling, unwilling to face the excitement it stirred. So, he shoved it down, locking it away in the darkest corner of his mind, the same place where all his uncomfortable thoughts and emotions had gone for years.

"Whatever am I to do?" Miss Bennet's large eyes glistened with a look of quiet desperation. "I came to you straight away to see if you could advise me."

Isaac paused, thinking. "There's only one thing to be done. Return home and explain to your mother that you were mistaken."

"Mistaken?" She raised an eyebrow, her tone laced with doubt. "That I accidentally thought I had accepted a proposal of marriage?"

Isaac's jaw tightened. "Or you could tell her the truth, that you lied. But I doubt that would go over any better. Either way, the truth must come out — quickly, before things get any worse."

Miss Bennet looked down, her fingers twisting together in a nervous dance. "The truth is like a delicate flower," she said softly, her voice almost a whisper. "It must be carefully tended to. Could not this flower be strong enough to withstand..." She lifted pleading eyes, her hands clasped before her in entreaty, "a small period of neglect?"

Isaac's brow furrowed, his pulse quickening. "A 'small period'?" His voice grew tight with confusion. "What do you mean by that?" Isaac felt his determination wavering. Never had someone quoted himself to himself before. Miss Bennet had listened when he spoke about Grannie Tiffin's lessons, and here she was using those sacred words against him. He should be angry, but instead, he was touched.

Miss Bennet watched him, a trace of hesitation in her eyes. "A fortnight, perhaps?" Her blush deepened as she looked away, her hands pressed together in a silent plea. "Just long enough for a bit of... courtship. We could spend a little time together, and after a few weeks, I could call it off amicably — say we just didn't suit."

Isaac's thoughts froze. He stared at her, caught between disbelief and an odd sense of tenderness. Never had he heard such a plan laid out so casually, and yet, there was something in her expression that made him want to believe in it — for her sake.

"I... I don't know," Isaac murmured, his heart thumping in his chest. He could feel his resolve waver, a sensation that had never occurred when he was with Grannie Tiffin. Here, however, with Miss Bennet, every instinct he had seemed at odds with the simplicity of her request. Was it possible to make such a thing work? To pretend, for just a short time, that they might be more than they were?

Isaac resumed pacing, his boots scraping against the cobblestones. A fortnight. Feigning engagement to Miss Bennet. Why did the idea thrill him so? He clenched his fists in frustration. It was a dangerous game, one that could bring about consequences far worse than a bruised reputation.

Already, he was walking a thin line with Mr. Phillips. His position as a law clerk was tenuous at best. If he lost it, he would have nothing — no job, no place to stay, nothing but the cold streets of Meryton and a life in tatters. A stranger in a strange town, thrown out with no safety net beneath him.

Yet, despite the risks, the possibility of an alliance with Miss Bennet's family could buy him time — time to prove his worth in Mr. Phillips' eyes. He could learn the role, adapt to office life, and perhaps make something of himself. He had no choice but to grasp at whatever opportunity came his way.

He stopped, turning to face Miss Bennet, who was watching him intently. Her large eyes held a mixture of hope and trust, and something else, something soft and vulnerable, that made Isaac's chest tighten. He sighed deeply. This was madness, but sometimes, madness was all one had to cling to.

"This is a bad idea," he muttered, more to himself than to her. "I want to say that right off. But... I suppose the flower of truth could bend in the wind for two weeks."

Miss Bennet's face brightened immediately, her eyes sparkling with gratitude. "Oh, thank you, Mr. Tiffin! You don't know how much this means to me."

Isaac exhaled sharply and stepped closer to her, pointing a finger toward her with emphasis. "Only two weeks, mind. Then we break it off and go on with our lives. No more of this nonsense after that."

Her smile faltered slightly at his firmness, but she nodded eagerly. "Of course, Mr. Tiffin. Just two weeks."

Isaac's chest tightened again. He couldn't understand why he felt so conflicted. This wasn't supposed to be personal. It wasn't supposed to mean anything. But the way she looked at him — the way she made him feel like perhaps he mattered, if only for a short while — was a complication he hadn't anticipated. Still, there was no turning back now.

"You probably should call me Kitty," she said, her face lighting up with relief as she smiled at him.

Isaac blinked, taken aback by her suggestion. "Use your pet name? I could never do that. Um... What is it short for?" The mere thought of using a nickname made him uneasy. The back of his neck prickled with warmth at the very idea.

"Catherine," she replied, holding out her hand for a shake.

Isaac hesitated for a moment before shaking her hand. "Then I shall call you... well... Catherine," he said, his voice steady, though his heart was beating faster. "Should you prefer Tiffin or Isaac for me? I answer to both."

"Isaac?" she repeated, her smile softening as she considered the name. "The Bible patriarch who worked fourteen years for love? Yes, I should like to call you that, Isaac."

Isaac smiled awkwardly, his grip tightening on her hand as they shook. He had no intention of breaking the bones of a lady, but his hand was large, and he was aware of how strong he was. "Two weeks," he said, grounding himself with the reminder.

"Two weeks," she agreed, and in that moment, everything between them shifted. It was done.

Fog wrapped itself in moonlight as the sleepy town of Meryton slumbered. On the outskirts, a sleek black carriage waited in the stableyard of the Black Friar's Inn. Its horses had long since been unhitched, their owner having spent the better part of the day in the taproom, drowning his sorrows.

Blackwell stopped counting the pints after the third. There seemed little point in keeping track anymore. The morning had bled into afternoon, and the evening into night, yet still he sat, wallowing in the shadows of his misfortune.

That damned girl. She had ruined everything. What was the point of courting a chit if she was already spoken for? She could have mentioned that in the damned letter she sent to her sister. It would have saved him time, and the money he had borrowed from Wickham to rent the carriage and buy himself some decent clothes. All for nothing. Now he was deeper in debt than when he began.

Blackwell slammed his tankard onto the scuffed table, imagining it as the face of that blonde brute who had claimed the prize before him. What he wouldn't give to knock that jumped-up chawbacon down a peg or three.

And now he would have to crawl back to Liverpool and beg that blasted Merseyside moneylender for more time. If he didn't find a new scheme soon, Burke would send his goons after him.

As if summoned from the shadows, a pair of men cloaked in black materialized from the gloom at the other side of the taproom. They pushed their way toward him, their beady eyes fixed on his face in a way that made his blood run cold. He was out of time.

"Blackwell, fancy seeing you here?" said the shorter of the two, a man with a nasty scar running beneath his left eye. He settled into a chair, smiling thinly.

The second man loomed in silence, not bothering to sit. Instead, he stared down at Blackwell, his expression hard and watchful, as though awaiting a signal to tear him apart.

"I..." Blackwell stammered, his throat suddenly dry. The man who always had a ready retort found himself unable to speak. He cleared his throat, took a drink, and then tried again. "Gentlemen, how pleasant to see you here in this small corner of the world. I was just finishing up this pint before I set out on the road to go see your fine employer."

"Yeah, could be, could be. Or it could be you've spent the entire day here in this backwater booze parlor drowning your sorrows. See, we've been watchin' you, you oily cove. We know where you've been and where you're headed. It's time to pay up, one way or another. Hand over the blunt, or my associate here will take it out of your hide."

"There've been a few complications, gents, but I assure you, Burke's one thousand pounds is almost in hand. You know how slow these highbrows move. I just need another week, and all will be wrapped up nice and tidy."

"Another week, you say?" Scar asked, his yellowed teeth flashing in a grin that stretched like a crescent moon in the dim light.

"Indeed. We were just on the point of negotiations with her father, and then to the parson we were headed."

"Negotiations, eh? So not headed to Burke, as you said?" Scar's eyes narrowed, proving he wasn't as daft as he appeared. "No matter. We're here, and this is a nice enough town. Plenty of plum pockets to pick. We can wait another week, seeing as how we came all this way. But we'll be returning with Burke's blunt, or we'll be returning with pieces of you as payment. Either way, you have seven days to get your business done before we decide which payment we'll be bringing to Burke."

Seven days. That wasn't long enough to come up with a new scheme. He had to find a way to get his hands on Kitty Bennet's fortune—and he had to do it fast.

Apparently, he wasn't done with Longbourn after all.

Chapter Four

Kitty Bennet awoke feeling miserable on the day of the engagement dinner. The morning was beautiful, with a clear sky and the sun peeking through her bedroom curtains, but she couldn't appreciate it. Her eyes were swollen from tears, and she couldn't stop sneezing, making her feel as though she were at the bottom of a well instead of safely tucked in her bed.

At first, she tried to lie back down, but that only made her head throb more painfully. Reluctantly, she got up and took a large sip of Isaac Tiffin's anti-sneezing draught, hoping that it might work some miracle.

"Work, oh please work! I have so much to do today. I can't just lay about all day, oozing from my face!" Kitty was so uncomfortable, her eyes itching and her head pounding, she felt as if she might collapse entirely.

When the whirlwind that was Mrs. Bennet blew into her room, Kitty knew her life was over. "Whatever are you doing still in your bedclothes, girl?" Her mother never spoke quietly, and in her most indignant moments, her voice was practically a shout. She was currently very indignant.

"I am unwell, Mama," Kitty whimpered, instinctively covering her ears. "I need to rest."

"There is no time for rest! I need you downstairs, quick as you please to help with the preparations. I need flowers cut from the garden to fill all the vases I had put out on the dining table."

Flowers?! Flower arranging was the last thing Kitty wanted to be doing. Just the thought of stepping out into the garden, surrounded by so many things could make her...

"There is no time for rest! I need you downstairs, quick as you please, to help with the preparations. I need flowers cut from the garden to fill all the vases I had set out on the dining table."

Flowers?! Flower arranging was the last thing Kitty wanted to do. The mere thought of stepping out into the garden, surrounded by all those blooms, made her...

"Achoo!" Kitty sneezed loudly, barely managing to cover her mouth in time.

"My apologies, Mama, but I simply cannot help with the flowers. I must stay indoors today, as Mr. Tiffin suggested, and rest as much as possible before the dinner tonight. Could you assign me an indoor task instead?" She followed this request with another sneeze, just as forceful as the first.

"Vexing girl! This whole event is for you, and you cannot lift a finger to assist me? I need flowers, child, not sneezes!"

"It's the flowers that make me sneeze, Mama." Kitty explained, then blew her nose, hoping to breathe more easily.

"Useless! Very well, I'll have the maid make the flower arrangements, but it will be on your head if they're lopsided or full of weeds that make you sneeze even more. I cannot understand your selfishness, Kitty Bennet. Oh, my poor nerves! You'll be the death of me!"

Mrs. Bennet stormed out of the room in tears, her wails about her ungrateful daughter's abuse echoing down the corridor and all the way to the stairwell.

Kitty sank into the chair by the fire, wiped her nose, and closed her eyes. She knew she would pay for this later, but for now, she had the precious time she needed to rest. She resolved to make the most of her morning, prepare herself for the dinner, and pray that her sneezes would subside before the evening. One could only hope.

The time had come to prepare for the big event, but Kitty longed to return to her bed. She knew the engagement dinner had to be endured, but it felt like such a waste now that Mr. Blackwell was out of the picture. Still, she had asked Isaac to pretend to be her fiancé for two weeks, and as the dinner fell within that time frame, she was honor-bound to continue the ruse.

But Kitty deeply regretted making such outlandish claims to her sister, boasting about things that didn't exist—like dowries and fiancés. If only she had been more truthful, like Isaac Tiffin, who always told the truth, even when it was inconvenient. She wanted to be more like him, and she promised herself that she would be once all this nonsense was over.

Kitty surveyed her meager selection of dresses, wishing she had gone to the modiste with her mother when she had the chance. If she had, perhaps she could have persuaded her to fund a new gown—one designed for Kitty's proportions and coloring. Ever since their lessons had begun, Lydia had always been the taller of the two, and as a result, all the dresses she handed down to Kitty were slightly too long and required altering. Though Kitty had made do, altering them to fit properly, she couldn't help but feel it would have been delightful to have something made especially for her. Perhaps she could commission a wedding gown for the ceremony... but no, there would be no ceremony, she thought with a surprising pang of disappointment.

As it was spring, Kitty chose her yellow muslin gown embroidered with white flowers along the hem. She loved how the flowers seemed to dance when she twirled in this dress. It always made her feel like she was strolling through the garden—without the sneezes.

With no sisters available to assist, Kitty was left to style her own hair. Thankfully, the hours spent crafting coiffures for Lydia had paid off. In no time, she managed to weave a crown of braids that framed her face beautifully. A quick pinch to her cheeks for a bit of color, and she was ready to leave her room. But as she approached the threshold, a wave of nerves surged, halting her step.

"Kitty Bennet, it's only a dinner," she muttered to herself. "You will go downstairs, talk to your neighbors, and eat some good food." Talking and eating. That she could manage. Besides, she would see Isaac, and that was reason enough to press on.

When she reached the bottom of the stairs, Mrs. Bennet was already stationed in the foyer, hands on her hips, looking as though she'd been waiting for hours.

"Oh, there you are, finally! I swear you get slower every day. Now come stand here, and we'll be ready to greet our guests." The Bennet matriarch gestured to a spot in the center of the foyer, directly facing the front door.

"Yes, Mama," Kitty murmured and moved to the indicated spot. However, as a plinth in the foyer held a particularly pungent flower arrangement, she discreetly inched a few steps away, folding her hands demurely. Moments later, her father appeared, looking dapper in his best wool coat.

"You look very fine, Kitty," he said warmly, giving her shoulder a reassuring squeeze. "Just remember to breathe—but not too deeply. I hear that sort of thing will lay a girl flat."

Kitty managed a faint smile but could only nod. Her nerves were too tightly wound to muster a witty reply to her father's humor tonight.

The first guest arrived ten minutes later, just as Kitty's feet began to ache from standing so still. Mrs. Morris bustled into the room, her round cheeks flushed from the evening chill.

"Hello, Bennet family! What a grand sight you all present in your finery. I declare this is the perfect night for a party, would you not agree? The weather is fine, the roads are dry—why, there can be no impediment to a pleasant evening!" She continued without pause, shaking hands and chattering about the weather, the coach Mr. Bennet had sent for her, and how exceedingly thoughtful it was of him.

Kitty tried to follow the ramble but got lost somewhere between "pleasant evening" and "handsome of him." Smiling and nodding seemed the safest course, so she employed both liberally whenever Mrs. Morris glanced her way.

Mr. Bennet escorted Mrs. Morris into the drawing room, leaving mother and daughter to stand vigil at the household portal. Kitty felt oddly out of place, standing there as if they were a prestigious family at a grand estate. This wasn't a fancy dress ball, after all, and yet her mother insisted on this display. Kitty supposed her mother wished to proclaim their prominence in the neighborhood, and greeting the guests in such a manner was one way to achieve that.

"Stand up straight, Kitty," her mother chided, fussing with her posture as if it were a matter of life and death. "You want to look perfect when your fiancé arrives."

Fiancé—now there was a word Kitty could hardly get used to. She bit her lip, stifling the urge to sneeze as the growing scent of the flowers swirled in the air. She did her best to straighten her shoulders, even though they naturally sloped forward.

If only this night would pass without incident, then she and Isaac could part ways amicably, and Kitty could return to her quiet life as a spinster. She would miss spending time with Isaac, it was true, but it would be better to free him from all the lies she had forced upon him. He was such an honorable man; it was a shame to involve him in such deceit.

And then he was there, standing in the doorway like a monolith, his broad shoulders blotting out the lamplight behind him with their overbearing size. Instantly, Kitty felt calmer, her pounding heart settling into a different rhythm entirely. "Mr. Tiffin," she murmured as he approached. Behind him, she noted the arrival of her aunt and uncle, but she couldn't take her eyes off Isaac.

Isaac glowered from beneath drawn brows, a sure sign that he was uncomfortable. What a shame it was that, by being here, he made her feel so calm while he appeared so discomfited in return.

"Good evening," she repeated, extending her hand to him.

He stepped closer, shook her hand, then seemed to realize that it wasn't quite the right gesture for a lady. Instead, he leaned over her hand and kissed it. His lips were warm against her skin.

Kitty felt her face flush and, only then, registered the knowing smiles of her relatives in the periphery. "Welcome to Longbourn."

"Thank you for having me," Isaac replied, standing back up. His eyes, the color of a stormy sea, did not quite match the formality of his words. Kitty couldn't help but smile at the contrast.

She walked with him to the drawing room, trying to think of something innocuous to say. Instead, she settled on expressing what she truly felt, now that they had a moment away from her mother. "I want to thank you for the breakfast adventure. It was a wonderful experience I shan't forget as long as I live."

Finally, Isaac smiled. "I'm glad. Though, I must admit, your preference for coffee came as quite a shock. How can you stand the stuff?"

"I think I must like complex tastes that take a bit of work to appreciate," she replied lightly. As her words echoed in her mind, Kitty realized she meant them in more ways than one. Isaac himself was a complicated man—all sourness upon first meeting, with his blunt manner and unvarnished truths. But the more she got to know him, the more she uncovered the sweeter layers of his character beneath the gruff exterior. She had grown to appreciate him all the more.

Ten minutes later, Mr. Lloyd, Longbourn's closest neighbor, arrived to round out the party. He entered the drawing room on Mrs. Bennet's arm, his conversation effusive with compliments about the beauties of their home.

"I've always loved the aspect of my fields from this window. It has been an age since I saw the east knoll looking so fine. Would you not say so, Mr. Bennet?" Mr. Lloyd turned to inquire of their host, who murmured an almost unintelligible reply before resuming his conversation with Widow Morris.

Kitty found her father's reticence surprising. There was rarely a moment when Thomas Bennet didn't seize the opportunity for a witty remark. Still, she decided she had enough to concern herself with this evening without adding her father's unusually subdued behavior to her list of worries. She would have to trust that he wouldn't make things uncomfortable at the table.

A moment later, the butler entered to announce dinner. Kitty felt Isaac lean down to offer his elbow. Suddenly, it was her turn to be at a loss for words. She placed her hand lightly on his arm, took a steadying breath, and prayed nothing unusual or embarrassing would happen in the next three hours.

Isaac Tiffin should have been calm, especially with Catherine Bennet on his arm. Yet as he descended the stairs into the dining room, following Mr. Bennet's upright and purposeful stride, a sinking dread settled in the pit of his stomach. *It's just dinner,* he told himself, but the lingering gazes from the drawing room—judgmental and skeptical—clung to him like oil.

He didn't belong among them, not in their silks and pearls. He was a farmer, a man of the earth, no matter that he now worked for a lawyer. Isaac knew where he came from; he could hear the countryside in every syllable he spoke. And he knew exactly what these people were thinking: *What is this man doing with our Kitty?*

The strange thing was, he agreed with them.

There was no sense to be made of the events that had led him here: pulling out a chair for Miss Catherine Bennet, sitting beside her at an elegant table, laying a fine linen napkin across his lap, and praying the delicate chair beneath him wouldn't give way.

Under the table, Catherine placed a comforting hand on Isaac's, and his panicked thoughts stilled. He glanced over at her and saw her smile kindly, then caught the calculating look in her mother's eyes at the far end of the table. They had a performance to give tonight, to shield Catherine from any potential humiliation, and that mattered to him. She had shown him kindness, had looked at him not as an outcast but as a friend. The least he could do in return for her generosity of spirit was to sit at this table, break bread with her family, and do his best to make her evening go smoothly.

Unfortunately, this dinner was unlike any Isaac had ever attended. Three servants, a butler, and two footmen brought in a constant procession of dishes, placing them ceremoniously around the table. Isaac counted two soups, several dishes of vegetables, a haunch of ham, a rack of lamb, and an overwhelming number of side dishes—everything from mushrooms to rabbit pies. He counted over a dozen plates. Where was he to begin?

A sneeze sounded at his elbow, pulling Isaac from his thoughts. He looked over, instantly reminded of Catherine. Without a word, he removed his handkerchief and passed it to her. She took it gratefully, her expression warm with appreciation.

"Kitty, stop your sneezing," Mrs. Bennet snapped from the other end of the table.

"Yes, Mama," came a meek reply that set Isaac's blood simmering. Catherine Bennet should never be made to feel so diminished.

Isaac's eyes flicked to the flower arrangements dominating the table, their oversized blooms heavy with pollen. Without a word, he stood, lifted the nearest offending arrangement, and handed it to the butler. The man accepted it with a small nod, carrying it to a buffet along the far wall.

Isaac resumed his seat, ignoring the wide-eyed stares that followed his actions. Leaning toward Catherine, he murmured, "Better?"

She smiled through her sniffles, her eyes bright with gratitude. "Yes, thank you."

Around the table, conversation hesitantly resumed, and Mr. Bennet rose to carve the meat. Seizing the lull, Mrs. Bennet's voice rang out from her seat at the far end of the table.

"Tiffin, I made sure to order lamb for you. Mr. Bennet told me you used to run a sheep farm. A taste of home, eh?" She smiled triumphantly, her expression one of eager expectation, as though waiting for his praise.

Isaac felt a flicker of annoyance at her bluntness, but it was swiftly replaced by something warmer. The gesture, however clumsy, was undeniably well-meaning. "I'm deeply grateful, ma'am. 'Twas most thoughtful of you to consider my preferences. It's clear where your daughter gets her generosity of spirit."

This response was most pleasing to Mrs. Bennet, who flushed prettily and immediately began speaking of Isaac's fine manners to her sister. "Not at all the rough bumpkin I thought he would be," she murmured, her voice laden with pride.

Isaac turned his attention back to Catherine, noting the way she seemed to shrink from the attention, her gaze flickering to her plate.

"Which soup is your favorite?" he asked, watching her carefully, knowing her tendency to avoid decisive answers.

"I cannot say, sir," she replied demurely, her voice soft and uncertain.

"No soup then?" Isaac inquired, the corners of his lips lifting slightly as her eyes brightened just a touch at the question.

Before she could answer, Mr. Lloyd spoke up with his characteristic bluster. "Why, of course, you must have soup! It's the supreme culinary effort at any modern English dinner table. I myself take two bowls of soup each day—it keeps the humours well-lubricated, you see. Most efficacious for the circulation."

Isaac's gaze shifted between Mr. Lloyd and Catherine, then back to the soups. "Well, then, you simply must try both," he said, offering her the tureen that had been placed before him. He followed it up by reaching for a dish of vegetables and presenting it to her. "May I offer you the asparagus?" he asked, his tone softening into something almost playful.

"Please, I love asparagus," Catherine replied quietly, a small twinkle lighting her eye. The warmth in her expression encouraged Isaac, and he continued offering her the next few items with the same attentiveness. He took care to place only those dishes on her plate that seemed to genuinely delight her. By the end of the procession, Isaac found himself able to discern her preferences with ease. The slight crinkle at the corner of her eyes told him whether she truly wanted an item or was merely being polite.

Isaac couldn't help but feel the evening was shaping up to be quite productive. Not only had he spent the meal bolstering Catherine's reputation, but he had also continued their culinary adventures from the morning—a private connection he cherished amid the evening's formalities.

When the ladies rose to withdraw to the drawing room, Isaac found himself caught off guard by the shift in tradition. He looked up to see Catherine's perennial smile turn apologetic as she followed the others. Evidently, this was how things were done in grand houses, though he felt her absence keenly. He could only hope the men would finish their business quickly so they might rejoin the ladies sooner.

As the butler presented port and whiskey, Isaac accepted a glass of whisky, intending to sit quietly until the conversation—a mix of politics and topics he imagined were deemed unsuitable for ladies—came to its natural conclusion. However, he was quickly proven wrong.

The moment Mr. Bennet received his port, he turned to Mr. Phillips with an air of joviality. "I must tell you, your Tiffin here has been a great help to me."

Isaac froze, his whiskey halfway to his lips. He swallowed hard, then set the cut crystal tumbler down on the table, trying not to grip it too tightly.

"Has he now?" Mr. Phillips responded, his tone mildly curious as he sipped his own port. His gaze flicked to Isaac, who squirmed under the sudden attention. "I was under the impression he was unable to assist with your books."

"That may be true," Mr. Bennet conceded with a chuckle, "but he was invaluable in the service of a stuck calf."

Isaac's embarrassment gave way to genuine curiosity. "How are they, sir?"

Mr. Bennet raised his glass in a toast-like gesture toward Isaac. "Alive and thriving, thanks to you. I've never seen a farmhand strong enough—or determined enough—to save a twisted calf. You did well, and I'm most heartily grateful."

Mr. Phillips tilted his head, his interest piqued. "Didn't you help out over at Preece's place as well?"

"I did, sir," Isaac managed to croak, his voice rough with nerves. "I was hoping to gather more information about the missing will." Finally, he took a long sip of his whiskey, the burn of the liquor steadying him as it chased away his dryness.

"Excellent idea. Farm with the farmers to get them off their guard. Tenants will never speak to me, no matter how I try," remarked Mr. Lloyd from his corner, swirling his port. "Devil of a time getting accurate information out of them. I've learned never to ride out on my hunters when I want the truth. I should hire you, Tiffin, to work my land sometime."

The mercenary gleam in Mr. Lloyd's eyes set Isaac on edge. He straightened slightly and replied, "I'm afraid I already have employment under Mr. Phillips."

"And we're happy to have him," Mr. Phillips interjected smoothly, raising his glass. "There's no better man for connecting with our clients, and he's just begun. I look forward to seeing what the future holds for you, my boy."

Isaac blinked, taken aback. For the first time, he realized that he, too, was curious about the possibilities. Life in Meryton had turned out to be far less of a nightmare than he had feared when he first arrived. If he could just unravel the mystery of the missing second will—and, of course, survive the remaining week of his faux engagement—he could imagine a real future for himself here in Herefordshire.

The thought of Catherine Bennet crossed his mind. He pictured the way her eyes crinkled with amusement as she smiled over her plate of asparagus. Without realizing it, he smiled into his drink.

"Same here, sir," Isaac said, his voice steadier. "I am eager to see what's to come."

Kitty arrived at the breakfast table the morning after the engagement dinner to find her mother absent.

Her father glanced up as she entered and, seeing the questioning look on her face, simply said, "Nerves." He returned to reading his paper, clearly unfazed. It seemed that his wife was overtaxed from the previous evening's exertions.

Kitty settled into her usual spot and ate her breakfast as she always did, yet a secret smile played on her lips as she surveyed the room. The dining room was unchanged from any other day, but in her mind, there was a man seated beside her—one who seemed to tower like a giant, offered her dishes with consideration, and even moved flowers out of her way so she could breathe without sneezing. It had been the most delightful evening she had ever experienced, and she expected it to remain a cherished memory for the rest of her life.

Though she drank her usual oversweet tea and ate buns and jam as always, the sustenance she felt now was one of the heart, nourished by the warmth of her memory. When she finished her meal, she bid her father a good day and made her way upstairs to check on her mother, wondering if she needed anything.

"I am worn to the bone, girl!" Her mother wailed the moment she saw her daughter step through the boudoir door. "Slaving away to entertain the neighbors, how will I ever recover?"

Kitty hurried to her mother's bedside, gently taking her hand. "There, there, Mama. It was a very successful evening. Everyone in attendance thoroughly enjoyed themselves. You can rest easy knowing that."

Mrs. Bennet sighed with evident satisfaction. "It was successful, wasn't it? Two full removes, jellies, pies, and the lamb that Mr. Tiffin seemed to relish immensely. Did you notice he helped himself to a second serving? I must say, your man is a hearty eater. I shall never fear leftovers with him at table."

Kitty felt a pang of guilt but managed to suppress the wince that threatened to crease her expression. Isaac wouldn't be dining at Longbourn again—not if their plan succeeded. Unwilling to stir any disappointment, she swiftly changed the subject. "Is there anything I can do for you, Mama, while you're recuperating?"

"We have the thank-you visits to perform," Mrs. Bennet said, her voice gaining a determined edge. "Can you begin with Widow Morris and your aunt? Perhaps Mr. Bennet will escort me to see Mr. Lloyd.

I don't suppose we need to visit Mr. Tiffin to express our gratitude. It was as plain as day that your company was thanks enough for his presence." She preened with pride. "Imagine—five daughters married! We must start planning the wedding. Where will you live? Somewhere in Meryton, I expect, but that's a conversation for the men to settle, I daresay. Oh, the banns! We must contact Reverend Halsey to have them called this Sunday. There's so much to do!"

Kitty's panic rose with every new item added to her mother's growing list. Mrs. Bennet chattered on, oblivious to her daughter's mounting distress, detailing plans for visits to the modiste for wedding clothes, the menu for the wedding breakfast, and more. By the time she began listing potential names for grandchildren, Kitty had reached the end of her patience.

"I'll prepare to call on Aunt Phillips and Widow Morris and leave you to rest, Mama," Kitty said, forcing calm into her voice. "I'll check on you when I return."

"There's a good girl. I always did like you, Kitty. Never gave me a moment's grief like the others," her mother replied, her tone softening. She mumbled a few more endearments before settling back with her tea and her ever-expanding plans.

Kitty left the room, her heart a whirl of emotions. The strain of her imaginary engagement weighed heavily on her, wrapping her in anxiety so intense it made her scalp prickle. Yet amidst the turmoil, her mother's words lingered. *I always did like you, Kitty.*

It was the first time she could recall receiving such praise from her mother, and the glow it sparked warmed her deeply. As she replayed the moment in her mind, the heaviness lifted, and she skipped along the corridor and down the stairs, as if carried by a breeze.

Bonnet and gloves in place, Kitty stepped out into a world transformed by her buoyant mood. Even if she had walked into a blizzard, she would have danced through the snow, imagining it as a cascade of flower petals. Her happiness lit her path as she set off toward town, deciding to visit Widow Morris first since the woman was known to be an early riser. While it wasn't the usual hour for calling on neighbors, Kitty and her family had never stood on ceremony with their friends. She was certain of a warm welcome. Nothing could dim her spirits today.

Upon knocking, Kitty was promptly admitted into Mrs. Morris's front room, a cozy parlor decked with lace curtains and an abundance of embroidered cushions. She settled onto the settee, her gloved hands folded neatly in her lap, and waited for the mistress of the house. At the sound of footsteps in the hall, she rose and turned to greet her hostess with a bright smile—only for it to falter when Mariah Lucas bustled in.

"Mrs. Morris is indisposed. I apologize, but she's unable to come down at the moment," Mariah said, her voice brisk but polite.

"Why, hello, Mariah," Kitty stammered, her thoughts spinning. She knew she was forbidden to speak with the Lucases, but how could she avoid conversation when one of them was unexpectedly thrust into her path? "I—I'm surprised to see you here."

Mariah smiled kindly. "I can imagine. I had come to visit Mrs. Morris when she began to feel poorly in the midst of our conversation. I had just finished helping her up to her bed when I heard the knock upon her door."

"Ah, that explains it. I'm so sorry she took ill. Is it anything serious?" Kitty tugged at the fingers of her gloves, her body stiffening with concern.

"No, I don't think so. I believe she was simply tired after the excitement of last night. I'm sorry she'll miss your visit. She spent our time together telling me all about the wonders she experienced at

Longbourn. Mrs. Morris mentioned your engagement. Allow me to wish you happy."

"Thank you, Mariah. I greatly appreciate your kindness."

Silence stretched between them like a languorous cat, filling the space until Kitty grew decidedly uncomfortable. After a moment, it was Mariah who broke the stillness.

"I've missed our talks, Kitty. Won't you tell me about your betrothed?"

"Mr. Tiffin is the best of men," Kitty replied sincerely. "He's a bear when you first meet him, but it's all bluster. Underneath, he's the kindest, most honest person you could ever meet. I am grateful to have met him." As she finished speaking, she realized she meant every word. Isaac was honest and good, and he had only made her life better since entering it. Perhaps he would marry Mariah once their ruse was over. But why did that thought leave her with an inexplicable sense of sadness?

Mariah smiled warmly. "I can see how much you care for him. He's a fortunate man to have won your heart, Kitty. I hope you both have decades of happiness."

"I should go," Kitty said, still lost in her thoughts. "I'll call on Mrs. Morris another time."

"Of course," Mariah replied. "Let me come with you. I must head home myself."

The two left the Morris house together, stepping onto the street almost in unison. Mariah seemed on the verge of asking the question that burned in her eyes, but instead, she simply said, "I do miss you, Kitty," before turning to head toward the business district and the shops on Church Street.

Kitty watched her go, her heart heavy with a mixture of guilt and sadness. Guilt, because she knew she had hurt Mariah by not inviting her to the engagement dinner, and sadness for the imagined future romance between her friend and Isaac Tiffin.She turned down the road leading out of town, her eyes drifting past the people she passed. By the time she reached Longbourn's gravel drive, she was feeling very low indeed.

⁂

Isaac had the pleasant surprise of encountering his employer on his way out of the breakfast room that morning at the Phillips townhouse.

"Morning, Tiffin," greeted the head of the household, his perennial twinkle in full force.

Isaac nodded. "It's a pleasure to see you this morning, sir," he said, and he meant it.

"Come, sit with me while we eat. It's thanks to your miracle cream that I'm able to rise before noon, so we might as well take advantage of the time saved and have a bit of a talk." Together, they walked into the dining room, where Mr. Phillips planted a kiss on his wife's hair.

"Good morning, my love," he said as he made his way to his chair. "Would you mind terribly if the men of the house discussed business?"

"I've just finished my coffee," replied his wife, standing. "So, I'll make myself scarce. You two have a good day at work, and do try to be home by six."

"Of course, my treasure," Mr. Phillips grinned as his wife left the room. "Marvelous woman," he mumbled to Isaac. "I don't know why she chose me."

"Chose you, sir?" Isaac asked, taking a seat.

"Most assuredly. No matter what any man tells you, it's a woman who chooses who she wants to wed. She's been making decisions for me ever since." A footman laid his master's breakfast before him, and Mr. Phillips began to eat with gusto.

"Now, let's talk about the Preece situation," Mr. Phillips changed the subject as he cut a rasher of bacon. "What's your opinion on all the goings-on up there?"

"As I see it," Isaac began, "Mr. Preece made a will several years ago and entrusted it to your practice, but when he fell ill, something made him change his mind. He wrote a new will, and it became the subject of some argument between his two sons. There are few reasons why a man would change his will, that I know of."

"What is the reason here, do you think?"

Isaac considered his words carefully. He did not think this was the time to blurt out his opinion on Young Dave Preece and how he had acted when Isaac first visited the farm. Then again, Young Dave appeared to be hiding something, and it wasn't hard to guess what.

"I think the revised will that the elder Mr. Preece denies knowing about has been hidden or destroyed because he disagreed with its contents."

"Did Norman mention anything about the second will when you spoke with him the other day?"

"He said he didn't know about it. He did recall an argument his father had with Young Dave not long before the patriarch's death, but he didn't know what it was about, beyond hearing the word 'will' amidst all the arguing." Isaac felt Norman was a trustworthy man. He did not feel the same way, however, about his brother.

"Hmm... it's a quandary, but I think you have the right of it. A second will was drafted, but before I could get up there to make a copy, the poor man passed. What would you do if you were in my shoes?"

"I would send me back to that farm to have a look around when the brothers weren't there."

Mr. Phillips nodded over his breakfast. "I agree. There's no need for you to come into the office. Head over to the farm directly and see if you can't get to the bottom of this pickle. If you can find the will, that would be best, but if not, come back and we'll make plans to head over together."

"I would rather not throw my weight around when you've been doing so well, but it might come to that. David Preece was a stubborn fellow, and his boys were cut from the same cloth. I look forward to seeing how you get on, my boy. And, thank you again for what you've done for my back. I feel like a new man."

Isaac took his leave of Mr. Phillips and made the short walk to the stables, his thoughts consumed with how best to get the information he needed. He desperately wanted to succeed, not only for his reputation with Mr. Phillips, but also to uncover the truth. This fragile truth had been trampled almost beyond recognition, and it was up to Isaac to see it saved.

The stablehand recognized him as soon as he stepped into the yard. "Heading out to the farm again, sir?" He had already picked up a bit and was on his way to harness Mabel.

Isaac waited until the stablehand returned with the horse to reply. His mind wandered as he waited, until it caught on a man leaning against a window on the opposite side of the street. His overly casual manner seemed out of place amidst the bustling Meryton street, so full of people coming and going.

"Aye, heading out to visit the Preeces once again. Here's hoping I'll have more success this morning than before."

The stablehand made quick work of hooking Mabel up to the cart. While he waited, Isaac's eyes wandered across the street. The man was still there, still leaning, still casual. Isaac noted the jagged scar slashing under his left eye. The man locked eyes with Isaac, brashly nodded, and pushed off the building before strolling away. Unnerved, Isaac wondered if he should follow, but then the stablehand tossed him Mabel's reins, and his original errand supplanted his curiosity.

The drive was largely pleasant, though Isaac noticed storm clouds rolling in at a swift pace. He would most likely be driving back to town in the midst of a spring rainstorm. A bit of rain never hurt him, though, so Isaac thought nothing of it.

He passed Longbourn, and his thoughts turned to Catherine Bennet. Though, if he were honest with himself, his musings were never far from her these days. He wondered what she was doing. Did she rise early, or was she a languid sleeper, preferring to spend her mornings abed? The dangers of that line of reasoning presented themselves immediately, so he changed mental course and reminded himself of how beautiful she looked the night of the engagement party. There, that was safer ground to tread.

The sky was completely grey by the time Isaac reached the top of the hill that overlooked the Preece farm. He thought again of Catherine and their conversations the first day he had passed this spot. A smile came unbidden to his lips. She was such an open girl, easy to talk to. She never looked at him like an ogre, something to be feared. To her, he was simply Isaac, a man who spoke his mind too quickly. There was something altogether wonderful about being known not as a monster, but finally as himself. He had the distinct feeling that, were it not for his friendship with Catherine, his life in Meryton would have turned out entirely differently.

Instead, here he was in Herefordshire, carving out a place for himself among good people who seemed to enjoy having him around. Mr.

and Mrs. Phillips seemed to appreciate his company, and Mr. Bennet had expressly thanked him for his assistance.

A familiar scarred figure leaned against a tree at the top of the hill, and suddenly Isaac's calm happiness shifted into alarm. The same man who had watched him on the streets of Meryton was inexplicably here, smiling up at him as his cart approached. Isaac slowed as he neared the tree, his jaw clenching as anxiety bubbled within him.

A second man stepped into the middle of the road, broader than the first and a head taller. Isaac was forced to stop the cart, lest he run the man over.

"Good morning, sir," said the first man, still leaning under the oak. "We'd like a moment of your time."

The second man took hold of Mabel's bridle, distracting Isaac as the carthorse emitted an affronted whinny. His companion pushed off the tree in the same manner he had pushed off the building in Meryton, coming to stand beside Isaac and casually removing a pistol from his pocket. "Step down, if you'd be so kind. Our boss would like to have a word with you."

"And who would your boss be?" Isaac asked, his hands balling into fists as he complied. Down on the ground, he was still two heads taller than the brigand, but a gun certainly evened the odds.

A horse clopped out of the trees, a hunter of uncertain breeding but good stock. "I am," said its rider, a triumphant glint in his dark eyes.

"Blackwell," Isaac growled between clenched teeth. "Say your piece and let me be on my way."

"I'm afraid your errand will go unfulfilled, Tiffin," the rider sneered. "You see, I have plans for you, and they don't include trotting down to that farm." Blackwell smirked, his handsome face contorting with smug self-assurance. He nodded at the second man, and Isaac barely had time to register the billy club before it came crashing down on him, plunging his world into darkness.

His last thought was one of curiosity: What did Blackwell want with him?

CHAPTER FIVE

The rain began mid-morning, just as Kitty was finishing another letter to her sister—this time free from lies. She spoke of general things: the weather, the family's health, and explained that they had held a small dinner for local friends, which was all true. She did not mention Isaac, nor the faux engagement, for she knew it would be over by the end of the sennight. In the end, it was a letter thankfully free from falsehoods, but also free from excitement.

When Kitty first noticed the rain, she thought little of it. Then she remembered the picnic and Isaac's reaction at the mere thought of approaching the water. He hadn't explained why he detested it, but it was clear something traumatic in his past had engendered such a strong aversion—especially for someone from Cumbria, a county known for its beautiful lakes.

The storm strengthened throughout the day, and with it grew her concern. Did Isaac get equally upset about rain? It had been a mostly dry spring, so Kitty hadn't yet seen how he handled poor weather. She needed to check on him, to ensure he wasn't struggling, particularly as the storm intensified into a downpour. Wasn't he heading to the Preece farm again? Surely he wouldn't be out in the rain.

She needed to find out news about Isaac, and there was one place she could always count on for information. Kitty called for the carriage, bundling herself up in her wool cloak and sturdiest bonnet. She would visit her Aunt Phillips, as she hadn't had the chance to make her return visit the day before. It was a little late for calls, but she was family.

The drive between Longbourn and the Phillips' abode was blessedly short, giving her little time to dwell on her worry. With the rain pouring down so fiercely, she nearly slipped on the cobbles as she hurried to the townhouse's front door, seeking shelter on the stoop. The butler almost betrayed his surprise at her unexpected visit, so strong was his reaction.

"Is Aunt Phillips in for callers?" Kitty asked, breathless.

"Who is it, Watkins?" came Mrs. Phillips' voice from the sitting room.

"It's me, Aunt," Kitty responded.

"Well, let her in before she drowns!" rang out her aunt's voice.

Kitty stepped inside, shedding her wet outer clothes and grateful for the warmth of the townhouse. She entered the sitting room and crossed to kiss her aunt.

"Hello there, my girl. What a surprise to see you on a day like this. This is no weather for visiting."

Kitty's worry bubbled to the surface, and she couldn't keep up the pretense any longer. "I came to inquire about Isaac. Have you heard anything of him? Is he well?"

Mrs. Phillips smiled kindly as she retook her seat. "He was well when he left with my husband this morning. I'm sorry to say your uncle returned earlier than expected, complaining of his back."

"Oh, I'm so sorry to hear that. I know he suffers terribly when the weather turns poorly."

"Ever since he was thrown during that cursed hunt a decade ago. Stormy days are his nemesis, I'm afraid. He came home and went straight up to bed. Here, let me ring for tea, and you can explain why you're concerned about Mr. Tiffin."

Kitty had been so worried that she'd forgotten her promise to Isaac. His difficulties with water were something he didn't want known, particularly by his employer. She assumed that this prohibition would extend to his employer's wife. But now she had blundered in and opened her mouth without thinking. Should she lie about why she was concerned? She knew Isaac valued honesty, but she couldn't very well break her promise to him just to speak the truth. She settled for honesty without betraying her word.

"I'm afraid knowledge was entrusted to me in confidence, and I cannot share it. I am sorry to have barged in here. I admit I let my emotions get the better of me."

"Do not worry, child. It is natural to be concerned about the man you love."

Love? Did she love Isaac? That was absurd. Kitty was fond of him, surely, and she respected his values, but that was all. "I just want to ensure he is in no difficulty," she responded lamely.

Thankfully, a moment later, the tea things arrived, and her aunt busied herself with pouring out and distributing the cake. She cut a third slice and sent it up to her husband along with a cup of tea. "This will make him feel a bit better," she explained to Kitty. "Bernard loves cake."

As they began to settle in and enjoy their cups of tea, Kitty heard a knock at the front door. She exchanged a curious glance with her aunt.

"My, aren't we just the most popular house in Meryton!"

The butler opened the door, and through the open doorway to the foyer, Kitty heard him speaking with a man in a low voice. The door was opened wider and then closed. A moment later, the butler stepped into the sitting room. "A Mr. Preece to see Mr. Phillips."

"See him in, Watkins," commanded Mrs. Phillips, setting down her cup and saucer. She stood to welcome the newcomer. "You are very welcome, Mr. Preece. How can I help you?"

Kitty recognized the man as the younger of the two Preece brothers, a tall, wiry figure named Norman. Seeing him here in the Phillips' sitting room set her teeth on edge. It could not be a coincidence that she had been worrying about Isaac heading out to the Preece farm, and here was Mr. Preece himself, standing before her.

"My apologies for interrupting your tea time," Mr. Preece said, creasing the brim of his sodden hat in two well-worn hands. "I've come on a matter of some urgency. Is Mr. Phillips available to speak with me?"

"He is not, I'm afraid," Mrs. Phillips replied. "He's unavailable to callers at this time. Is there something I can assist you with?"

Norman looked from Kitty to Mrs. Phillips and back again. "No, ma'am. I thank you, but this isn't a matter for ladies. I bid you good day."

Anxiety rose in Kitty's throat, so powerful she thought she might choke on it. She shot to her feet. "Mr. Preece, do you have news of Isaac Tiffin by any chance?" Her fear made her brave, and she hoped with all her heart that her worry was unfounded.

Kitty's world narrowed to a single point as Norman nodded, his expression grim. "I do. I'm afraid he's been kidnapped."

The world around Kitty seemed to blur into a haze. Everything she saw and heard grew distant, as if swallowed by fog, and one word echoed endlessly in her mind: *kidnapped*.

"I'm sorry," she said, her voice trembling so much she could barely recognize it. "Could you please explain?" She gripped the arm of the sofa, trying to steady herself, desperately hoping she had misunderstood. But when her eyes met Mr. Preece's, that fragile hope shattered.

"My dear?" Her aunt was instantly by her side, handing her a handkerchief, though Kitty's eyes remained dry. It was as though she had lost the ability to feel anything at all, not if Isaac Tiffin was no longer part of her world.

"My apologies, Miss Bennet. It weren't my intention to upset you so," Norman said, his voice laced with regret. "This is why I sought Mr. Phillips. This is no matter for ladies to worry over."

"This is exactly the kind of matter I should be concerned about," Kitty shot back, anger rising inside her. Why was it that no one ever thought she should be included, even when things that deeply affected her were at stake? "I ask you again to explain what happened. Don't mince your words, Mr. Preece. I need to know what's happened, and quickly."

Seeing Kitty's determined expression, Mr. Preece shut his mouth around another protest and nodded reluctantly. "Yes, ma'am. I was working out in my fields this morning, repairing a dam that had burst along the river by one of our paddocks, when I noticed a group of men standing in the middle of the road up on the hill above our farm. Do you know the spot?"

"Yes, I know it. I've visited your home before. Please, go on." Kitty gripped her handkerchief tightly in both hands, twisting the fabric to keep from shouting. Why couldn't he just get to the point?

"Well, there were two men standing under the oak on the hill, talking to another man on horseback. Then the man on horseback and one of the others moved into the brush behind the tree. I was about to write it off as some kind of odd business meeting—strange as it seemed—when Mr. Tiffin drove up in his horse and cart.

"He got down and spoke to the man in the road for a moment, but then the other two emerged from hiding. I think one of them struck him over the head, because Mr. Tiffin crumpled like a dropped cloth onto the road. A minute later, two of the men brought up a shiny black carriage, tossed him inside, and drove off. The third man, a gentleman on a fine hunter and smartly dressed, simply rode away as if it were nothing more than a casual morning outing."

Mr. Preece dropped his head, guilt and misery weighing down his shoulders. "I would have come straight away, miss, but right then my cows broke through the dam I was repairing. Cor, it took me all afternoon to round them up again. Exhausting work, that was, I can tell you! When I finally got home, though, Mr. Tiffin's cart and horse were in my farmyard, and I remembered what had happened. So I came as quick as you like to see Mr. Phillips, since Mr. Tiffin works for him. But when I got to Mr. Phillips' office, it was already closed. I don't know who took Mr. Tiffin, but they must have had nefarious intent to knock him out cold like that."

Kitty shot to her feet, pacing as her thoughts raced. A black carriage sounded familiar, but she struggled to place it. A gentleman's equipage, certainly—but where had she seen it before? Black, shiny... "Mr. Blackwell! He owns a carriage just like the one you described."

"But why would Mr. Blackwell wish to harm Mr. Tiffin?" Aunt Phillips asked, her expression bemused.

"I am not certain," Kitty lied, "but I must go and speak with my father." She turned to Mr. Preece. "Will you come with me, sir? It may be that my father knows better than I what questions to ask you."

"I will," he said, setting his hat firmly back on his head. The brim dripped large, wet drops onto his shoulders, leaving his wool coat spotted with dark patches.

Kitty embraced her aunt. "Thank you for the tea." She wanted to say more but held her tongue in front of Mr. Preece.

Her aunt gently pulled Kitty back, holding her at arm's length to look into her eyes. "You came seeking news of your Mr. Tiffin. Now you must find him. I will pray for you."

Kitty nodded resolutely, then stepped into the hallway to retrieve her cloak and bonnet. The Bennet carriage still waited on the street, so she led Mr. Preece to it and climbed inside. "Take me home, Peter," she commanded, unconcerned by how brusque she sounded. Now was not the time for niceties.

Mr. Preece settled across from her, holding his hat in his hands and remaining silent. It was a wise choice, for Kitty doubted she could maintain her composure if she were forced to speak. She had lied to her aunt just now, as she had lied to so many others over the past few days. Oh, if only she had been honest from the start, none of this would have happened!

It was her fault that Isaac was in danger. Her falsehood about the dowry had drawn the mercenary Mr. Blackwell to Meryton. Then, persuading Isaac to agree to that sham engagement had placed him directly in Blackwell's path. Isaac was everything good and honest, and now Kitty's endless deceptions had endangered him.

What sort of woman had she become? She had been raised to be honest, to read her prayer book on Sundays alongside her sisters. Goodness knew Mary had moralized enough in her presence to last a lifetime. And yet, here she was—sinking so low she barely recognized herself. All this deceit, and for what? To appear more respectable in her sister's eyes? To shield her reputation when she turned down Mr. Blackwell's proposal?

No more. Kitty would not continue down this path. From this moment, she resolved to emulate the qualities she most admired in Isaac: his honesty and courage, even when it meant enduring discomfort or humiliation. She wanted to become the kind of person he could be proud to know. Whether or not he forgave her for the turmoil she had caused, she would beg his forgiveness the moment they met again.

But first, she had to ensure his safety. Isaac needed to be freed from Mr. Blackwell's clutches. It was time to speak with her father.

Kitty alighted from the carriage, Mr. Preece trailing close behind. As she approached Longbourn's front door, the ever-faithful Griffiths swung it open with practiced efficiency.

"Miss Bennet, I am very glad to see you safe." His gaze swept over her sodden form before landing on the man behind her, his expression hardening with cautious scrutiny.

"This is Mr. Preece," Kitty explained, shedding her cloak. "He is my guest. Please ensure he is given hot tea and something to eat." Turning to Mr. Preece, she loosened her bonnet strings and added, "I will need to speak with my father alone, if you don't mind."

Mr. Preece shook his head. "Don't worry about me. I'll be here when you need me—I'm not going anywhere in this weather."

Kitty offered him a small, grateful smile before heading straight to her father's book room. This was his haven, the one place he could escape the cacophony of family life. Raising five daughters with one of the most tempestuous wives in the county made such a refuge essential—if not daily, then hourly.

Unsurprisingly, she found him seated in his usual chair, deeply engrossed in a volume on herd management. He didn't even glance up as she entered.

"Kitty," he acknowledged without lifting his eyes, calmly turning a page.

"Father, I must speak with you. Something dreadful has happened to Mr. Tiffin, and he needs our help immediately."

Surprise lifted Mr. Bennet's eyebrows as he finally peered at her over the edge of his book. "I can see this is distressing to you. Sit down, child, and let's hear what you have to say."

Kitty perched on one of the chairs across from her father, her fingers twisting together in her lap as she wrestled with where to begin. She decided to lead with the most pressing news. "Mr. Tiffin has been abducted."

"Tiffin? That seems improbable. Have you seen the size of him?" Mr. Bennet smirked, clearly unmoved by her evident distress.

"Mr. Preece saw strangers knock him unconscious and throw him into a black carriage. Please, Papa, we must do something!" Anxiety boiled inside her, barely kept at a simmer only by sheer force of will.

"Now, Kitty," her father replied with maddening calm, "Mr. Tiffin is the strongest man I've ever met. I'm sure he's already handled those ruffians and is back with the Phillips', regaling them with tales of his adventure."

"No!" Kitty shot to her feet, hands balled into fists at her sides. "You don't understand. He's been kidnapped by Mr. Blackwell, and it's all my fault!"

At this, Mr. Bennet set his book aside and stood, wrapping an arm around her shoulders. "How could you possibly be involved in this? You're a young lady, not some criminal mastermind. This sounds like the kind of trouble men stumble into on their own. It will sort itself out, mark my words."

Kitty felt frustrated tears burn her eyes. Her father wasn't listening and wouldn't understand unless he knew the full truth. Well, she had vowed that she would stop telling lies, did she not? Now was as good a time as any to begin down the road toward honesty. "Mr. Blackwell has kidnapped Isaac Tiffin because he believes I have a dowry of 1000 pounds." Just saying the words aloud calmed her nerves. The weight that had been pressing down upon her heart lifted.

"Why would Blackwell think that?" Her father stepped back, folding his arms across his chest. His brow furrowed deeply with confusion.

"Because I told Lydia that you had given me a dowry so I might finally be married," Kitty admitted, her voice trembling with shame. She dropped her head, unable to meet his gaze. "I wrote to her about this fabulous amount you had supposedly bestowed upon me, and Mr. Blackwell must have overheard it while visiting his cousin."

"Wickham," Mr. Bennet said, his voice laced with disdain. "Nothing good ever comes from that family." He sighed, but his expression hardened as he pressed further. "How does this connect to Mr. Tiffin?"

"Mr. Blackwell wanted that dowry for himself," Kitty explained, her voice quieter now. "When I turned down his suit, he became furious. He wouldn't let it go. So...I lied again. I told everyone I was already engaged."

"To Tiffin," Mr. Bennet interjected, his tone sharp as understanding dawned. His arms dropped to his sides as he finally grasped the full extent of her actions.

"Yes," Kitty said, barely above a whisper. "It was a fake engagement, meant to last just two weeks—long enough for Mr. Blackwell to leave town. Then I planned to quietly end it without tarnishing my reputation. But now he's back, and he seems determined to remove Isaac from the picture entirely. Perhaps he thinks that if Isaac disappears, he'll have another chance to press his suit and claim my supposed dowry."

"Oh, Kitty, you foolish girl!" her father said, his gaze sharp with disappointment, mirroring the self-loathing she carried.

Kitty hung her head as hot tears spilled down her cheeks. "I know, Papa. I've done nothing but hurt Isaac, and he's the best of men. Now he might die because of me! Please, Papa, we must save him!"

When she dared to glance up, she saw her father's expression soften. His eyes grew distant, glazed with thought—the unmistakable look of Mr. Bennet deep in contemplation. Kitty clung to the small flicker of hope that stirred within her aching chest. Perhaps, just perhaps, not all was lost.

After what felt like an eternity, he finally spoke. "It took courage to confess to your lies, Kitty Bennet. I must admit, I'm impressed. And now, I will do the same—I shall own up to my mistakes. There's only one man I know with the reach to track down Blackwell."

Kitty blinked through her tears. "But how? By now, they could be anywhere!"

"Not if Blackwell intends to woo you again. He'll want to ensure that his rival is firmly out of the way."

At this, Kitty let out a small, choked sob, the weight of her guilt threatening to overwhelm her.

"Come now, child. All is not lost yet," Mr. Bennet reassured her, a rare note of determination in his voice. "If I'm right, Blackwell hasn't gone far. He's likely still in Meryton, ensuring Isaac remains 'disposed of.' So, we shall pay a visit to Sir Lucas and hope he'll forgive me for my ill temper this past week. Like you, I'll have to summon some bravery and speak the truth. It may be enough."

"Mr. Preece came with you, didn't he?"

Kitty nodded, her voice catching. "Yes. He said he'd stay and help us whenever we needed him."

"Good. Then let us head to the Grange and do some groveling. Come, Kitty Bennet—it's time to save your man."

"But he's not my man, Papa," Kitty protested, her voice trembling. "I told you—it was all a lie."

"One thing at a time, dear girl. One thing at a time."

The Grange, home to the Lucas family, stood perched on a gentle rise on the south bank of the river. In fair weather, it command-ed a picturesque view, overlooking the winding waters as they me-andered toward Meryton. But this was no such day. Sheets of rain lashed the land, reducing the surrounding countryside to a blurry haze. When the carriage finally halted before the house—a handsome structure with its striking Tudor half-timbered facade—the double doors swung open. The travelers hurried inside, where all greetings and exchanges of identity, thankfully, took place within the warm, dry confines of the entryway.

A silver-haired butler took Mr. Bennet's card to the dining room, where the family was still at table. Moments later, Sir Lucas emerged, striding toward them with hand extended. "Bennet! I am surprised to see you all on such a beastly night. What brings you here, especially in this weather? Do you have urgent business with me?"

"I do," Mr. Bennet replied. "Might we speak privately? The matter is quite pressing."

"Of course. This way." Sir Lucas gestured toward a tastefully furnished sitting room just off the main hall. Kitty trailed behind Mr. Preece and her father, quietly settling herself in a corner to remain unobtrusive.

"I must begin by assuring you," Mr. Bennet said, "that I wouldn't interrupt your evening unless the matter were of the gravest importance. A life is at stake, and your assistance is critical in averting disaster."

Sir Lucas's expression grew solemn. "Say no more, Bennet. You have my full support. Whatever resources I can provide are at your disposal."

"Thank you, Lucas. Mr. Tiffin, an employee of my brother-in-law Mr. Phillips and fiancé to my daughter, has been abducted by a rogue intent on doing him harm. We suspect he's somewhere near Meryton, but as I lack meaningful contacts in the area, I thought..."

"That my shipping concern could be of use," Sir Lucas interjected, stroking his chin. His primary business interests in Herefordshire lay in a thriving shipping enterprise, one so instrumental to the nation that the Prince Regent had made him a Baronet. "Yes, my men know the streets of Meryton as well as their own palms. I'll send word immediately for them to begin searching for Tiffin. Do you have any idea where we should focus our efforts?"

Kitty's thoughts turned swiftly to the day Isaac confided his unease with large bodies of water. He had begged her to keep his secret. But now, having vowed always to be truthful, she wrestled with the dilemma of honoring his confidence while helping save his life.

Then, another memory surfaced: the sight of Mr. Blackwell that same day. It was likely the scoundrel had overheard Isaac revealing his fear. Blackwell might exploit that knowledge. Sharing this with her father could be the key to finding Isaac swiftly—it might mean the difference between rescue and disaster.

Could she reveal his secret, knowing it would bring him shame and likely make him hate her forever? Kitty pressed her hands to her chest, her eyes squeezed shut as she wrestled with the choice. Betray his confidence to save his life—but lose his trust forevermore? It would have to be enough, she decided, just to know Isaac was alive. She could endure his anger and the loss of his kindness, so long as he remained in the world.

"I have information that might help," she said, rising and walking to where the men stood by the fire.

"What is it, child?" her father asked, angling his stance to include her in their circle.

Kitty took a deep breath and plunged ahead. "Isaac—Mr. Tiffin—is deathly afraid of drowning. I believe Mr. Blackwell may have overheard him sharing this with me. If so, he could use that fear against him. I would suggest starting your search..." She faltered for a moment, the image of Isaac trapped where his worst fears might come true seizing her thoughts. "At the river," she finished, her voice steadier than she felt.

Sir Lucas crossed swiftly to a lady's writing desk near the windows and scrawled a note. He rang for a footman. "Have one of the stable-hands deliver this to Jack Fletcher immediately," he instructed. "The address is on the back. I need Fletcher and his men searching near the river, without delay. The man's life is in grave danger."

The footman trotted off toward the back of the house, and Sir Lucas returned to their circle of confidence.

"I will go with them," said Mr. Preece. "The more eyes, the better."

"We should all go, I say," pronounced Sir Lucas. He called for the butler to bring the carriage around. "Kitty dear, stay here with the ladies in case someone turns up with Isaac. If he shows, send word to my warehouse – my staff will know where to find me."

He turned a curious eye on Mr. Bennet. "I must ask, why the change of heart, my dear man? I had thought our friendship lost for-ever when you didn't invite us to your little gathering." He extended a hand in friendship toward Kitty's father.

Mr. Bennet took the hand gratefully. "I admit, when I heard you scuttled the land sale between Lloyd and I, I went a bit red. Couldn't stand the thought of such betrayal, so I cut all ties, even fired that steward you had recommended. Now it seems like a small thing to lose a friend over. Tonight my daughter reminded me that sometimes we need to see past our own pride to what really matters."

"I had nothing to do with that sale failing, man. Who told you that?"

"Mr. Blackwell, come to think of it. Are you saying the blackguard lied?" Kitty's father glowered in a way that made Kitty fear for Mr. Blackwell should he ever show his face again.

Sir Lucas nodded. "It appears so. The land Lloyd tried to sell was entailed, Bennet. He tried to sneak one past me, but I've been a mag-istrate too long to let something like the sale of land you don't own slide. So sorry that put you out, man." He clapped Mr. Bennet on the shoulder, smiling, "I must say, it's been a while since I saw you in a lather. It's not a good look."

By this time, the carriage was ready, and the footman's note had been retrieved. Kitty hugged her father and decided it was best to occupy her mind by visiting with the ladies of the Lucas house. She barely drank the tea they provided and heard even less of the friendly questions Mariah asked. Her thoughts and her heart were far away in Meryton, with a man deathly scared of water, facing a flooded river. She hoped her father would find him before the waters claimed him.

Isaac Tiffin awoke waist-deep in a rushing river with no memory of how he came to be there. His head felt thick, as if it were filled with wool, and his tongue was dry even though he was surrounded by water. He moved his limbs slowly and found that, while his legs were free, the icy water covering his lower extremities inched up his torso with every passing moment. His arms, on the other hand, were bound behind him with thick ropes, connected to something that anchored him to the stonework behind him.

His first thoughts were of confusion, but then the sheer terror hit him as he realized the nightmare of his situation. He was in the river, and with all the rain pouring down from the storm, it wouldn't be long before the–he looked up–bridge he was bound to would be covered over by the rising water. His greatest fears were going to be realized. He was going to drown.

He had felt this fear before but had staved it off for years by building barriers around his memories. Now the fear clung to his throat like a noose, breaking open his carefully constructed mental bulwark. Memories of the worst day of his life came crashing back into his mind with the force of the flooding waters around him.

Isaac and his parents had gone on holiday after a successful sheep slaughter, his father insisting they visit the Lake District and take in the beauty. It was supposed to be a carefree time, a break from the usual. But that holiday ended in the most unimaginable way. The accident—the one that still haunted his dreams—was seared into his mind. He could still hear his father's voice calling out, the frantic urgency, the way everything had unraveled in an instant. And then, the water. The rushing water that had swept them all away.

Isaac shuddered, feeling his breath grow shallow, as his heart began to pound harder against his chest. It had been years since that day, but the sensation of water rising, the suffocating fear of drowning, was as fresh as ever. His pulse quickened, his vision blurred with the rising tide, and he could feel the heavy weight of the past threatening to drag him under once again.

"Just because we're farmers don't mean we can't enjoy the wonders o' creation," his father had said in his booming voice. Isaac had been seven at the time and had worshipped his father and his larger-than-life personality.

They had journeyed north and taken a room at an inn with a view of the lake. The next day, they'd rented a boat. Isaac had been thrilled, it being his first time out on the water, and had eagerly reached out for a duck as it floated by. The boat tipped, and all three of them had ended up in the water as the unbalanced weight of the passengers capsized the craft. With the weight of her skirts, his mother sank beneath the surface.

"She can't swim!" his father had cried. "Stay with the boat, boy, and I'll go get her." His father had plunged in after her, while Isaac clung to the overturned boat with all his strength. His parents never resurfaced, at least not until a search party came the next day and dredged the lake. By then, it had been too late.

Isaac had been found hours later, shivering and sobbing, calling for his father. Ever since that day, he had avoided bodies of water larger than a puddle, even staying away from streams and ponds if he could help it.

But now his worst fears were realized. He was back in the water, feeling it tug at his booted feet, the sound of the rushing current deafening in his ears. His heart beat a rapid rhythm, thudding in his chest as he struggled to control his breathing. Panic made him nearly mad with fear.

It felt like days, but it was probably only a few hours. As the sun set, Isaac pushed himself as far up the grating behind him as possible. By the time the light had completely faded from beyond the footing of the bridge to which he was tied, the river had risen to his shoulders.

Choked by fear and frustration, with the water lapping at his chin, Isaac yelled in one last desperate call for salvation. "Help!" His words were immediately whipped away by the howling wind. It was useless, a waste of energy. He might as well give up and let the water claim him.

Had Blackwell done this, knowing that Isaac feared drowning? He must have, but how? Isaac's brain was too flooded with terror to concentrate, so he gave up thinking and simply closed his eyes, waiting for death to come on the waves.

"Tiffin!" A voice called through the storm, and Isaac opened his eyes. Was he hearing things?

"Here! I'm here in the water! Help me!" he cried with all the desperation of a man at the end of his rope—because he was.

A moment later, feet splashed into the river next to the bridge. Figures waded over to where Isaac was tied, and then hands pulled at the ropes binding him, sawing through them with a knife, and finally offering him freedom. Several hands pulled Isaac from the water, and he was free. Free!

His legs were numb, and the men who rescued him had to help him climb onto the shore, where he collapsed, gasping for air. He heaved great lungs full of the rainy night, coughing into the mud as the adrenaline began to ebb.

If he had had any energy left, Isaac might have cried from sheer relief. Instead, he scrambled away from the river's edge. When he finally felt strong enough to stand, he stumbled toward a group of men gathered beneath an awning.

He recognized a few of their faces. "Mr. Bennet? Mr. Preece?" he croaked, his voice raw from the ordeal. He bent over, bracing his hands on his knees, as relief surged through him like a flood.

"Thank you," he managed to say over the roar of the rain and the ragged rhythm of his own breathing. "Thank you."

CHAPTER SIX

Kitty Bennet spent the better part of the stormy evening pacing the drawing room at the Grange. She tried her best to be polite, nodding, smiling, and replying to the conversation around her, but her mind refused to settle. Everything that had happened in the past week raced through her thoughts, most of it centered around one particularly tall, former farmer. What a dreadful mess she had made of everything!

Tea failed to calm her stomach, and conversation could not soothe her frayed nerves. She found herself making a mess of the lovely carpets Mrs. Lucas had painstakingly laid down only a month before, in an effort to refresh the style of her grand yet comfortable home. Kitty noticed the tracks her boots left in the floral patterns, but she couldn't stop herself from pacing. Her body craved release, while her emotions had none.

The more time passed, the heavier her heart grew. No comfort came to ease her worry. As one hour turned into two, despair began to take root. What if her foolish lies had led an honorable man to his death? Did Isaac know how much she cared for him? Did he know he was cherished, even above all others? Would he face a watery grave unaware of Kitty's true feelings?

An hour after sunset, the front door to the Grange burst open, and a huddled mass of mud and leather spilled into the foyer. Kitty halted her pacing and rushed toward the men as they shed their coats and blankets, shaking off the weather. There, between her father and Mr. Preece, hung Isaac Tiffin—battered, beleaguered, but alive.

It was all she needed to see. Kitty ran to him, throwing her arms around him with a cry of relief and fury. For several moments, she clung to him, her hands gripping his sodden coat with white knuckles.

"How dare you?" She seethed, her voice trembling with a mix of rage and relief. "You selfish, stubborn man! You, who never once bothered with politeness, decide now—of all times—to let someone abduct you? How could you!" Her hands were fists now, pounding helplessly against his chest, heedless of the mud and water that splattered over her.

"You absolute mountain of a man! How could you just allow a band of petty brigands to take you? You, who are twice the size of any reasonable person, suddenly decide to meekly let criminals carry you off? What gives you the right to let yourself be taken? I hate you! How dare you!"

She felt strong arms wrap around her, and she cried into his chest, sobbing intermixed with epithets. When she had spent all her rage upon him, she finally calmed enough to hear the murmurs he spoke into her hair.

"I'm sorry, Catherine," she heard, followed by, "Forgive me, dear," and then, finally, her favorite: "It's alright now, dearest."

Kitty looked up into his face. Despite the bruises mottling his skin, he was smiling. That smile sparked her temper all over again. "What are you smiling about?" she snapped.

"I never knew you had a temper," Isaac said, his grin widening.

"I didn't have one until I met you, you infuriating man. There's a whole host of emotions I've been keeping tucked away, but I promised myself I'd be honest from now on, and therefore..." She gestured dramatically, letting her exasperation speak for itself.

"Boom," he said softly, his laugh as gentle as the rain still pattering outside.

Kitty's anger dissolved into a defeated pout. "I was so very scared, Isaac. I thought I would never see you again."

The realization of their surroundings finally hit her. She was standing in the foyer of her neighbor's house, wrapped in the arms of her uncle's newest employee. A wave of embarrassment flushed her cheeks as she glanced around, noticing that the other men who had accompanied Isaac were nowhere to be seen.

Isaac caught her searching look. "I think they meant to give us some privacy." He couldn't stop smiling, and his sheer audacity set her teeth on edge.

"You and your smiles," she muttered, her pout deepening.

"You and your rages," he countered, his tone unshakably amused. "I quite like you like this, you know."

Kitty realized she was still standing within the circle of Isaac's arms. A sudden wave of self-consciousness washed over her, and she tried to step away, but his grip held firm.

"Let me go, you monster. I'm never speaking to you again," she said, pushing against him. It was as futile as shoving a wall of stone.

"A monster I am," Isaac said, his grin returning, "and selfish, and a brute, and"—his voice softened, teasingly— "hated. But that fire in your eyes, dearest, tells a different tale than your words."

He captured one of her hands against his chest, and Kitty's heart finally unclenched. Isaac was alive. A tentative smile began to bloom on her lips, but it faltered as he stumbled against her.

At last, he released her and brought a hand to his head, his expression turning pale. "I think I need to lie down, Miss Bennet," he murmured.

Alarm surged through her. She barely caught him as his knees buckled, easing him down to the floor as gently as she could. Panic rising, Kitty sprinted from the foyer into the drawing room, then to the dining room, and finally the kitchen. There, she found Sir Lucas and her father standing by the fire, their shirtsleeves rolled up against the damp.

"Isaac has fallen unconscious. Come help!" she cried, urgency thick in her voice.

The men followed her back to the foyer, where Isaac lay pale and still upon the floor. Sir Lucas immediately began issuing orders.

"We'll get him into a bed," he said, waving over several footmen. Together, they carefully lifted Isaac and carried him upstairs.

Mr. Bennet stepped up beside her. "I think it's best we return home, child. He'll be safe enough here. The worst has passed."

Kitty watched the men vanish around the next landing, then clenched her teeth, resolve hardening. He'd better be safe, or she'd kill him herself.

Isaac woke in an unfamiliar bedroom, his head pounding as if it might split apart. The furnishings around him were elegant, though slightly outdated, and it took a moment for him to piece together how he'd ended up there.

The memories came in fragments—first the bridge, then the water, and finally, the rescue. His thoughts shifted to something far more pleasant: Catherine Bennet, her fury ignited in the Grange's foyer. He smiled faintly, recalling how she'd raged at him for "letting himself be abducted"—as if he'd had any say in the matter.

Her fiery outburst had been an unexpected revelation. Catherine Bennet would never be an easy woman to live with, but by George, he wanted to try. Once he recovered from nearly drowning, he'd head straight to Longbourn to speak with her father.

For now, though, he needed to heal. Despite his broad shoulders and formidable stature, Isaac felt as fragile as a newborn kitten. Hours spent battling the river's currents had drained him more than he'd realized. And then there was the memory of his near-drowning—a terror that still coiled through his veins like venom. He'd have to conquer that fear if he ever wanted to avoid coming face-to-face with his nemesis again.

Come to think of it, his nemesis wasn't really fear after all but the man who had tried to kill him. Blackwell—the oily snake-in-the-grass who had slithered back into Isaac's life. And for what? To get his hands on Kitty's dowry, Isaac supposed. What a heap of trouble that girl and her lies had caused.

Still, no lasting harm had been done, beyond a few bruises and the nasty lump on the back of his skull. Isaac would heal. And then, he'd pay a visit to that blackguard and show him the meaning of true fear.

A knock at the door interrupted his thoughts. When Isaac called out, the door opened to reveal Mr. Bennet's smiling face.

"You're awake, lad. Glad to see it," said the older gentleman, stepping inside and crossing to the bedside. He shook Isaac's hand, his grip firm and surprisingly strong for a man of his years.

When Isaac had first met Mr. Bennet, he'd thought him no different from the other idle country gentlemen—men who lounged about hunting and shooting while their tenants toiled to fill their coffers. But he had since learned otherwise. Mr. Bennet was the sort to work his land alongside his tenants, and Isaac respected him all the more for it.

"Thank you for your rescue efforts, sir," Isaac said without preamble. "If it weren't for you and your men, I'd be floating face down in the river by now."

Mr. Bennet frowned. "What happened to you was terrible, son, and I'm glad I was there to help bring you back hale and hearty. I've recently learned the reason for Blackwell's attack, and I must say—it's a wicked act, all for so little gain."

He must be referring to the supposed dowry of a thousand pounds Catherine had claimed to possess. Isaac furrowed his brow, worry for her relationship with her father pressing heavily on his mind.

"It wasn't Miss Bennet's fault that scoundrel came looking for an easy mark," Isaac said firmly, determined to shield her from blame. "Blackwell is a snake, and snakes will always target the weakest prey. Once I'm back on my feet, it'll be my top priority to find him and his lackeys and deal with them."

"About that," Mr. Bennet said, rocking back on his heels, his expression thoughtful. "I have an idea about how we might handle Blackwell—if you're willing to hear me out."

Isaac's eyebrows rose, his interest piqued. "Go on, sir. If you have a plan, I'm all ears."

"We have an opportunity here," Mr. Bennet began. "Blackwell doesn't know you survived his attack. You haven't been seen at your workplace or your townhouse. For all he knows, you're an obstacle he's eliminated. He's too arrogant to consider his plan might have failed. We shall—and we can use that arrogance against him."

He walked to the window, gazing out over the park surrounding the Grange. "Here's what I propose: we keep you hidden here under Sir Lucas's care. Meanwhile, I'll wait for Blackwell to return and resume his so-called courtship of my daughter. When he does, we'll capture him. It may take some patience, but I suspect Blackwell needs that money quickly. He'll show up sooner rather than later. What do you think?"

Isaac's eyes dropped to the counterpane covering his knees, his teeth clenching as anger surged through him. "Allow Blackwell to court Catherine? I'd rather be tied back under that bridge."

"Not allow," Mr. Bennet corrected firmly. "Never that. Just see it as the bait to lure him into our trap."

"There's much to dislike about this plan of yours," Isaac grumbled. "I hate the idea of you putting yourself in danger, sir. And I hate even more having to hide like a scared child from the man who tried to harm me."

Mr. Bennet returned to stand beside the bed, his expression resolute. "This is our chance, my boy, to rid ourselves of him for good. Until he abducted you, I had no idea how dangerous that monster truly was. Now I must do all I can to protect my daughter from him."

Monster. The word struck Isaac like a blow. He'd been called a monster his entire life—from the day he lost his parents to the moment he stepped foot in Herefordshire. People had always regarded him as something unnatural. Even Catherine had called him a monster just the other night—but for reasons entirely different. "I would see your daughter saved from harm at any cost," Isaac said quietly, his voice steady, "even to my pride."

He looked up at Mr. Bennet, the anger ebbing away as determination surged through him, flooding his veins with purpose. "Let's put your plan in motion."

Rufus Blackwell arrived a week later, impeccably dressed in green superfine and adorned with a ruby stickpin. His dark hair was combed to perfection, his boots gleamed in the spring sunshine, and even the wheels of his black lacquered coach shone from meticulous polishing. He stepped down with effortless grace, carrying a bouquet of hothouse blooms in one hand. After straightening his immaculately folded cravat, he rapped confidently on Longbourn's front door.

Mrs. Bennet greeted him with effusive delight, her eyes lighting up at the sight of the flowers. "What a gentleman you are! Such exquisite blooms—I shall have them put in water at once." She called for a servant, handed off the bouquet with an air of importance, and ushered Blackwell into the drawing room with practiced hospitality.

She took a seat and gestured for him to do the same, her smile overly wide, revealing a bit too much tooth. "I'm sorry to say, Mr. Blackwell, that our Kitty is not at home just now. Such an attentive niece she is, always visiting her dear aunt each week. Would you care to wait for her return? I'm sure she'd be dreadfully sorry to miss you."

Blackwell hid his irritation behind a polite bow, his expression never wavering. "I've actually come to see Mr. Bennet on a matter of important business," he said smoothly, letting the emphasis on *important* linger just long enough for her to catch his meaning. Then, with a practiced smile, he turned on all his considerable charm.

"Oh! Well then, I won't keep you a moment longer. Come see me once you've had your very important conversation, sir, and we shall talk specifics." Rising with determined cheer, Mrs. Bennet crossed the room and, without waiting for an invitation, took Blackwell's arm. Though he had not offered it, she clasped it firmly and led him down the stairs and along the corridor, her momentum leaving him no choice but to follow.

They stopped before a closed door. Without so much as a knock, she pushed it open and announced, "Mr. Blackwell is here to speak with you, Mr. Bennet. I'm sure you'll want to hear what he has to say."

She gave Blackwell's arm conspiratorial pat, her smile teetering on the edge of a giggle, before leaving him awkwardly on the threshold of her husband's domain.

Inside, Mr. Bennet, being the out-of-touch recluse that he was, sat behind his desk, immersed in a hefty tome. At the intrusion, he looked up and offered a genial smile. "Ah, Mr. Blackwell, come in, come in. I have one matter to address, and then we'll have a nice, long talk."

He quickly scrawled a note, rang for a servant, and handed the missive over. "Take this to the Grange. Ensure the goods are delivered immediately and bring them back with you," he instructed. The servant nodded and disappeared with brisk efficiency.

Blackwell lingered near the doorway, uncertain where to begin. Deciding on civility, he strode forward and extended his hand. "I'm very happy to see you, sir," he began warmly.

Mr. Bennet crossed to the drinks tray. "Brandy?" he offered.

When Blackwell nodded, Mr. Bennet poured two generous glasses. Handing a snifter to his guest, he added, "It's good to see you again. The house has been rather dreary without your visits. Where did you run off to?"

Blackwell wracked his brain for a suitable excuse. "A sick aunt required my attention," he said smoothly. "I received word a few weeks ago and felt it my duty to attend her."

"And is your aunt improved?" Mr. Bennet asked, settling into a chair by the fire.

Blackwell took the seat opposite him. "She is, I thank you. As soon as I saw her on the mend, I felt compelled to return to Longbourn and its many enticements."

"It's commendable for a young man to be so devoted to family," Mr. Bennet remarked, raising his glass.

Blackwell offered his most self-deprecating smile. "And how is your family, sir? I trust they are all in good health?"

"Oh, we're carrying on as usual. Not much of note happens in sleepy little Meryton, as you know. Life here remains much the same." Mr. Bennet paused, then asked with an air of casual interest, "Have you heard anything from my son-in-law since your departure?"

It took Blackwell a moment to understand whom Bennet was referring to. When he realized the subject was Wickham, he shook his head. "Not as such. Wickham isn't the sort to reach out unless he needs something. He's had an easy time of it, with the Darcys paying his way in the world."

The warmth of the brandy emboldened Blackwell, and he leaned forward, his voice tinged with bitterness. "Everything handed to him, Wickham never remembers family unless they can serve his interests. He fails to appreciate his good fortune. I, on the other hand, have had to make my own."

"And is that why you're here?" Mr. Bennet asked, his expression a mixture of curiosity and scepticism. "To seek your fortune?"

Before Blackwell could respond, a knock at the door announced the arrival of a servant. The man stepped inside and leaned close to whisper something to his master.

"Ah, my delivery has arrived," Mr. Bennet said. "Leave it in the hall; I'll tend to it when I'm finished here."

With the servant gone, Blackwell resumed. "The day I met Miss Kitty Bennet was the day fortune finally smiled upon me."

Mr. Bennet tilted his head, a faint smile playing on his lips. "Ah, yes, my lovely daughter. Does it not concern you that she was previously engaged?"

"I left too quickly to share my truest feelings with her, Mr. Bennet. I cannot blame her for seeking solace elsewhere. It's my understanding that the relationship you refer to ended when the man disappeared?" Blackwell finished his drink, steadying himself for the real reason he had come.

Before he could continue, however, a voice spoke from behind him. "And where did you hear that?"

The uncultured tone froze Blackwell mid-thought. His blood turned to ice as he recognized the voice of a man he believed was dead and gone.

Slowly, Blackwell turned, only to find Isaac Tiffin standing in the doorway. The man's towering frame filled the space, and his eyes gleamed with a dangerous intensity.

Shock immobilized Blackwell for a moment, but instinct soon took over. Driven by sheer panic, he leaped from his chair and bolted for the door.

Tiffin moved with terrifying speed, blocking the exit with his massive frame. He seized Blackwell effortlessly, his grip as unyielding as iron. "Oh no, you're not getting away that easily," Tiffin growled. "We've got some unfinished business, you and I."

Still seated by the fire, Mr. Bennet spoke with infuriating calm. "I'm afraid, Blackwell, that your sources were a bit unreliable. Never mind. We'll get everything sorted out in due time."

Blackwell thrashed against Tiffin's hold, but it was hopeless. The man towered over him by at least two heads, and his strength was insurmountable.

"Blast it!" Blackwell spat, his voice a mixture of frustration and fear.

Tiffin dragged Blackwell unceremoniously out of the room, his iron grip giving no room for struggle. Down the corridor and out the front door they went, where Blackwell's rented black carriage stood waiting. A footman held the door open, his expression betraying no surprise at the scene unfolding before him.

"Mind giving us a lift?" Tiffin asked, his tone almost jovial as he unceremoniously tossed Blackwell inside.

Climbing in after him, Tiffin pinned Blackwell against the corner with ease, gripping both of his arms in one massive hand.

Blackwell squirmed, but it was futile; Tiffin's hold was as unyielding as steel.

A moment later, Mr. Bennet joined them, settling into the opposite seat with unsettling calm. The carriage lurched into motion, the rhythmic clatter of wheels on cobblestones a grim reminder that they were headed toward a destination Blackwell was increasingly certain he did not want to reach.

For the most part, Isaac found Rufus Blackwell's sentencing to be rather dull. While it was immensely satisfying to see that snake finally get his comeuppance, the dry mechanics of the law held little interest for him. It was ironic, really, that he had ended up working for a lawyer.

For a man who loved the land as deeply as he did, it was an odd and sometimes frustrating profession.

Still, it was what his Grannie Smith had wanted for him. Not necessarily a life as a law clerk, but certainly a stable career—one that didn't depend on the unpredictable price of wool to keep food on the table. He understood her reasoning, even if he didn't fully agree with it. If it had been entirely up to him, he would have spent his days in Cambria, tending sheep and working the farm the way he'd been raised to do. But honoring his grandmother's wishes had always mattered more to him than his own desires, and so here he was.

These thoughts occupied Isaac's mind throughout the sentencing proceedings. Sir Lucas, serving as magistrate, delivered the list of offenses with brisk efficiency, the most notable being the abduction and attempted murder of one Isaac Tiffin.

Shame clawed at Isaac every time he remembered that scene on the hill above the Preece Farm. How had a man his size—mocked his whole life for being the closest thing to a real-life giant—been so easily subdued? He supposed the gun had something to do with it, but the memory still rankled. He hadn't been able to save himself from Blackwell's clutches, and that failure gnawed at his pride. The scoundrel must have known about his weakness somehow. What Isaac wouldn't give for just five minutes alone with that blackguard now.

Instead, he stood silently, watching as Blackwell was led away, his own gleaming carriage bearing him to the Highbury jail. There was some small comfort in knowing the Bennet family was safe from Blackwell's schemes at last. That would have to be enough—for now.

"Tiffin?"

The sound of his name broke through his thoughts. He turned to find Mr. Bennet watching him with a concerned expression.

"Yes, sir?" Isaac answered, shaking off the lingering cobwebs in his mind.

"Are you well? You've been through quite a lot these last few days," Mr. Bennet asked, his tone uncharacteristically earnest.

"Oh, I'll be fine. Never you mind," Isaac replied, brushing off the concern with a wave of his hand. "Takes more than a near drowning and a knock upside the head to keep me down."

Mr. Bennet chuckled softly but soon shook his head, a shadow of irritation crossing his face. "Blackwell played the fox in the henhouse, didn't he? Stirred up a storm of trouble—for what? A bit of coin?"

"Coin, sir?" Isaac asked cautiously, his stomach knotting with unease. Did Mr. Bennet know about Catherine's falsehood? The last thing he wanted was for her father's opinion of her to sour. It didn't matter what Mr. Bennet thought of him, so long as Kitty retained his respect."

Yes, dear Kitty told me about the little dance she's been leading us on these past weeks," Mr. Bennet said, his voice tinged with a mixture of fondness and exasperation. "If she'd wanted a dowry that badly, she needed only to ask. She never was one to speak up for herself, though. I ought to have seen that. If only—" He stopped himself, sighing heavily. "Well, I shouldn't blame her, all things considered. She wasn't the one spinning outright lies around here."

Isaac glanced at Mr. Bennet, noting the slump of his shoulders and the quiet resignation in his posture. The man who once seemed unshakable now looked like he carried the weight of his mistakes on a bent back. During his convalescence, Sir Lucas had confided in Isaac about Blackwell's deceit—how the man had manipulated Mr. Bennet over a doomed land deal, fracturing a friendship that had spanned decades.

"All is not lost," Isaac said gently, searching for words that might offer some solace. "Friendships, like barns, can weather storms. A good repair job—careful and deliberate—often makes them stronger than they were before. Shore up the roof, reinforce the walls, and it'll stand even sturdier next time."

A flicker of a smile softened Mr. Bennet's face, and the tension in his jaw eased. "You've a good head on your shoulders, Tiffin. I can always count on you for wise council." He paused, his gaze sharpening with curiosity. "Tell me, then—how would you handle my issue with the cattle? They're cramped on the land I have, grazing it bare. And now I know I can't buy more land from Lloyd. What would you suggest?"

Isaac straightened, his thoughts already turning to practical solutions. "You don't need more land, sir," he said with quiet confidence. "You need new methods. Have you heard of rotational grazing? It's a practice where you move the herd methodically through sections of your land. Each paddock gets its turn to rest and regrow while the cattle feed elsewhere. Done right, it improves both the land and the livestock."

"Another piece of solid advice," Mr. Bennet nodded, his approval evident. "It's no surprise that you're a wellspring of farming wisdom, considering your upbringing. Let me ask you, son—why are you still working for my brother-in-law when it's clear you're more suited to a life in the open air?"

Isaac met his gaze, taking a deep breath. "It was my Grannie Smith's last wish, sir. She wanted to see me settled in trade—living a life here, in her home county, not lost among the hills and crags of Cumbria."

"I see." Mr. Bennet's eyes narrowed with thought, then brightened as if an idea had struck him. "Well, I have a proposition that might benefit both of us. I need a steward, and it's clear you're better suited to life outside the office. What do you think? Would you consider accepting the position?"

Isaac froze, his heart pounding. The offer was nothing short of perfect. To be steward at Longbourn was to live the life his Grannie Smith had wanted for him—established, respected, with a hand in the land while still fulfilling his potential. It was everything he'd hoped for, and yet...

"Sir, I'd be honored," Isaac said, his voice steady, though the excitement inside him nearly overwhelmed him. "But there's something I must first address. I'm currently working on a case for Mr. Phillips, and I know his clerk would love to see me employed elsewhere. I'll have to speak with him before I make any commitments."

Mr. Bennet gave a knowing smile, one that hinted at his shrewdness. "A lawyer's business is never done until the ink dries, eh? I understand." He sat back, the expression on his face turning thoughtful. "But I'm sure there's something you could do, son—clever as you are. You've seen the way Blackwell's schemes played out, haven't you? Perhaps you've got a bit of a plan of your own."

Isaac's heart skipped a beat. Mr. Bennet's suggestion rang true. He'd learned more than just farming wisdom in his time at the law office. If he could use the same cleverness that had exposed Blackwell, perhaps he could resolve the mess left by the Preece brothers as well.

"Indeed," Isaac murmured, a determined glint in his eye. "I do have an idea, sir. I'll need to speak to Mr. Phillips first, but I believe I can help. It's time for me to turn the tables."

"Ever loyal, our Tiffin," Mr. Bennet said with a knowing smile. "As long as Phillips is agreeable, I'd be delighted to see you working at Longbourn. But there's one condition."

The dangerous twinkle in Mr. Bennet's eye made Isaac pause.

"And what might that be?" he asked, a trace of trepidation in his voice.

Mr. Bennet clapped him on the shoulder—no small feat, given the disparity in their heights. "You turn that fake engagement of yours into the real thing."

CHAPTER SEVEN

T he next morning found Isaac Tiffin guiding Mabel's little cart
through the Longbourn lands toward the Preece Farm. As he
neared the old oak tree atop the hill, a flicker of unease stirred in his
chest, recalling the events of his last journey down this path. But this
time, he wasn't alone, and the cheerful presence of Mr. Phillips beside
him brought a measure of reassurance.

Noticing Isaac's change in demeanor, Mr. Phillips clapped him
heartily on the back. "No need to fret, my boy. No ruffians will be
leaping from the hedgerows today. Let's not dwell on the past when
the present calls for our attention. Are you sure you've got everything
you need before we step into the lion's den?"

Isaac patted his coat pocket, the crinkle of paper audible even over
the hum of the cart's wheels. "Yes, sir. I'm ready this time."

He urged the horse forward, and the cart trundled down the familiar slope into the Preece Farm's yard. The sight stirred a pang of
nostalgia—it was a place so familiar it almost felt like home.

Dismounting the cart together, the two men approached the
kitchen door, which stood ajar, creaking gently in the morning breeze.
Isaac knocked on its weathered surface and stepped back, waiting to
see who would greet them.

A moment later, Young Dave appeared in the doorway, glowering up at Isaac with fists clenched tightly at his sides. "And what d'you want now?" he barked, his tone as sharp as the edge of a scythe.

Mr. Phillips, ever unflappable, stepped forward with a genial smile. "Good morning, Young Dave. We've come on a matter of some import and would appreciate a word with you and your brother, if you've the time."

Young Dave's demeanor shifted instantly, his posture softening from snarling watchdog to dutiful farmer. "Of course, Mr. Phillips. Do come in," he said, stepping aside and sweeping a hand toward the interior, opening the door wider.

"Would you happen to know where your brother might be?" Isaac asked as he ducked to enter the house. Farmhouses in England were seldom built to accommodate his size, and this one was no exception. He straightened carefully, the vaulted ceiling just allowing him enough space to stand, though he had to keep an eye on the beams sloping toward the far wall.

Young Dave's eyes flicked briefly to Mr. Phillips, his hesitation plain. After a moment, he nodded. "Yes, I'll fetch him. He should be over in the barn. Won't be but a moment." With that, he turned and strode back into the farmyard, leaving Isaac and Mr. Phillips alone in the kitchen.

Mr. Phillips cast an encouraging smile up at Isaac, a glint of mischief in his eyes. "Get ready, lad. The show's about to begin."

Norman Preece entered a few minutes later, offering firm handshakes to Isaac and Mr. Phillips before gesturing for them to sit at the worn kitchen table. The room felt crowded as Young Dave joined them, leaning against the wall with his arms crossed, his sharp gaze flicking between the visitors.

Isaac clasped his hands together on the table, taking a deep breath to steady himself. "I'm a newly appointed clerk working under Mr. Phillips at his law practice," he began, his voice low and measured. "This is my first time handling legal matters—papers and the like. Before I came to Meryton, I was a farmer." He paused, his eyes dropping to his hands. "That doesn't excuse what I did, but it might explain how I missed it." He let out a heavy sigh, the sound filling the tense silence.

Norman Preece leaned forward slightly, his kind eyes narrowing with curiosity. "Missed what?" he asked, his voice calm but probing.

Isaac hesitated just long enough to build the moment before reaching into his coat pocket. With deliberate slowness, he drew out a folded piece of paper, its edges yellowed with age. He set it on the table and looked up, his gaze steady but apologetic. "This."

The room's atmosphere shifted instantly, the weight of the revelation pressing down on them like a storm cloud. Norman stayed seated, his expression unreadable, but Young Dave reacted as though the paper were a venomous snake. He shot to his feet so quickly his chair toppled over, the clatter startling in the small space. Backing away until his shoulders hit the wall, his narrow face twisted in a mix of horror and fury.

"How can that be?!" he shouted, jabbing a trembling finger toward the paper as if accusing it of treachery.

"There was a second copy of the will sent to me," Mr. Phillips began, his tone even but firm. "Unfortunately, it was misfiled during Mr. Tiffin's... shall we say, haste to perform his new duties. It was uncovered only recently, during a thorough reorganization my senior clerk and I conducted to correct the, ah, chaos left in the wake of Tiffin's enthusiasm."

Isaac flinched, the pang of embarrassment cutting deep. He didn't need to feign the flush that crept up his neck as he murmured, "Again, I'm so sorry, sir." His eyes were fixed on the table as though it might provide some reprieve from his mortification.

Mr. Phillips smiled kindly, his demeanor softening. "No harm done, my boy. We threw you into deep waters and expected the back-stroke without asking if you knew how to swim. You got there in the end."

Before Isaac could respond, Young Dave exploded from his position against the kitchen counter. "You're lying!" he shouted, his voice cracking with desperation. "I burned the only copy myself!"

The words hung in the air like a thunderclap. As soon as he realized what he'd said, Young Dave snapped his mouth shut, his face draining of all color.

"You what?" Norman asked, his tone low and disbelieving, his kind eyes hardening as they locked onto his brother.

"I burned that damned will the night Father died ," Young Dave admitted, his voice faltering.

Mr. Phillips leaned forward slightly, his tone calm but edged with steel. "Does that mean you read its contents before you burned it?"

Young Dave's anger drained away, leaving only a hollow shell. He slumped against the counter, burying his face in his hands as if he could block out the judgment in the room. "Yes," he whimpered, his voice muffled. "Father gave everything to Norman. The land, the farm, all of it. It wasn't right, givin' the farm to the younger son while the older son gets nothing! What did he expect me to do—starve?"

Norman stood and moved to his side, placing a firm hand on his shoulder. "You're always welcome here, Young Dave. You know that."

"It's not the same, and you know it. A man needs something of his own." His voice carried the weight of betrayal, and Isaac felt an urgent need to ease his pain.

Isaac reached for the folded paper resting on the tabletop. Carefully unfolding it, he began to read aloud:

"'Mr. Phillips,

I've come to realize that my eldest son, David, has a longing for the sea. I suppose I'm to blame, sending the boys to visit my brother in Bristol when they were just young lads. He's carried this yearning all these years, and only now do I understand why he's always resented farming. His heart belongs to the ocean.

When my time comes, I ask you to send Young Dave to my brother Jedediah. I've written to Jedediah, and he'll be expecting him. My brother is a Crimper working on the Bristol docks. He'll know the right ship for an untrained lad hungry for adventure. Please, let my boy follow his heart.

Yours truly,

Dave Preece.'"

"Your father wanted both his boys cared for in the way he thought best," said Mr. Phillips into the heavy silence. "Norman loves the land—always has. And you, my boy, have been yearning for something different. He wanted to give you that chance."

Young Dave broke down, tears streaming freely as his younger brother wrapped him in a consoling embrace.

Mr. Phillips allowed them several moments to let their emotions settle. Finally, he rose and said, "Come see me in town in the next few days, you two. I have paperwork for the gifts your father left each of you."

"We will, sir," Norman replied softly. "And thank you—both of you. I suppose our father understood us better than we gave him credit for."

Isaac and Mr. Phillips left the house and were halfway back to town before either spoke.

"That was a clever bit of work back there, young Tiffin," said Mr. Phillips.

"Thank you, sir. I actually got the idea from watching Mr. Bennet handle things."

"Come to think of it, I received a note from Bennet recently. He says he wants to poach you, son, for his steward."

Isaac nodded, his words lingering in his mouth. "I will, of course, stay and work for you, sir. I have every intention of repaying your kindness."

"But is that what you want, my boy? What is your dream?" Mr. Phillips asked, casting a sideways glance at him and smiling at Isaac's confusion. "Not your Grannie's wish, but yours?"

That was a dangerous question, but since Mr. Phillips had posed it, Isaac couldn't help but give it honest thought. As they rode on, he pondered what he truly wanted out of life. He thought of mornings spent on the paddocks as a boy, the sheep standing in the mist. He thought of conversations with the Preece brothers in their humble kitchen. He remembered the time he'd helped birth a calf in the barn at Longbourn.

"I think I would like to work the land, living among people I care about. That's my dream."

Mr. Phillips nodded thoughtfully. "It's a humble dream, but a valuable one. I'm glad to hear you're finally being honest with yourself. It seems you'll be making another change, my boy. You know, your Grannie didn't send you down here to the Midlands for your security. She wanted your happiness."

Looking off at Longbourn in the distance, Isaac said with conviction, "I think I know where to find it."

Kitty knew she had to come clean to her mother. In her new life as an honest person, her mother was one of the last people who still believed her lies. But the thought of speaking directly to her mother, of confessing her falsehoods, twisted her stomach so much that she simply couldn't do it yet.

So, she made the decision to take the first step into her new, forthright life by clearing things up with Aunt Phillips. It was clear that, with all the commotion surrounding Isaac's abduction, her aunt must already know some of the truth, but it was time to set matters straight with her mother's sister.

She set out after a morning meal spent with her mother, who had been talking nonstop about wedding plans and making Kitty feel increasingly guilty. The sooner she set matters right with her mother, the better. She would speak to her today, she vowed, just as soon as she visited Aunt Phillips.

The morning was a little dreary, with fog curling over the fields that lined the road to Meryton. The village itself was just waking up, shops opening and homes bustling with activity. It was her favorite time to visit the village, when the promise of something great seemed to vibrate along the cobblestones.

She found Aunt Phillips still at the breakfast table. "I'm sorry to disturb you so early, Aunt. I hope I didn't wake you."

"Nonsense, child, you know you're always welcome. Family doesn't stand on ceremony. Come sit and have something to drink while I finish my meal." Aunt Phillips poured her a cup of coffee, adding cream and sugar before handing it to Kitty.

Kitty smiled as she took the cup, recalling her breakfast adventure with Isaac. Her aunt had been paying attention, even as she acted as chaperone that morning. Mrs. Phillips was always a clever sort.

"So," Aunt Phillips said, sipping her own coffee, "what brings you to see me this morning?"

Kitty clutched her coffee cup as if it were a lifeline. "I've come to set matters straight. There are some...falsehoods I've allowed people to believe over the last few weeks , and they've caused my friends and family a great deal of trouble. I'd like the truth to be known at last."

Aunt Phillips smiled kindly. "Does this explain why Isaac Tiffin was missing from our house for over a week?"

Kitty nodded solemnly. "It does." She dove into the story, starting from the beginning—with her letter to Lydia, where she had falsified a hefty dowry. She left nothing out, revealing the faux engagement, which eventually led to the worst night of her life—Isaac's abduction.

Throughout Kitty's explanation, Aunt Phillips interjected at key points. As Kitty finished her tale, Aunt Phillips reached the table and took her hand.

"You've been through quite a lot recently, dear Kitty. I want you to know that I forgive you for your falsehood. What's more, I understand them. No young woman wants to live a colorless life, and it's easy enough to embellish our lives in letters to those we admire. I hope you've seen, though, that it's better to create a more colorful life through good deeds, rather than pretending to have an advantageous existence."

"I do, Aunt, I very much do," Kitty smiled ruefully. "These lessons were hard-won, but I believe I've come out of these trials a better person. I only hope that the plan to end Mr. Blackwell's reign of terror concludes to the benefit of all—and swiftly. I hate to think of Mr. Tiffin having to hide away at Sir Lucas's home. He much prefers to be out of doors."

Aunt Phillips nodded knowingly. "Have patience, my child. It cannot be much longer. Now, have you heard the news?"

Kitty spent another hour with her aunt, enjoying the comfortable companionship as they exchanged neighborhood gossip—a welcome relief since, for once, none of it concerned her. At the end of the visit, she kissed her aunt goodbye and set off for home, heartened by Mrs. Phillips' kind reaction to her revelations.

The closer she got to Longbourn, the more trepidation coiled within her, knowing the time had come to have a similar conversation with her mother. Despite her desire to delay, Kitty had resolved not to let another day pass while her mother continued to believe those awful lies. With a determined mental shake, she crossed the threshold into her home and began her search for the matriarch.

To her surprise, her mother was not in the drawing room, where she usually spent her mornings mending and chatting with Kitty. Nor was she in her boudoir, her usual refuge when her nerves rendered life unmanageable. At a loss, Kitty ventured outside and found her mother in the cut flower garden, frowning thoughtfully over rows of daisies, roses, and peonies.

"Hello, Mama. What are you doing?" Kitty asked, genuine curiosity coloring her voice. It was unlike her mother to spend much time outdoors.

"Oh, Kitty! Excellent timing, my dear. I'm trying to plan what flowers might suit your wedding bouquet. So many of them make you sneeze, and no woman should be miserable on her wedding day. What do you think of roses? Do they tickle your nose at all?" She reached out, snipped a pale pink bloom from the nearest rosebush, and held it out to Kitty.

Kitty couldn't stifle the sneeze that erupted as she tried to smell the flower. Still, her mother's thoughtfulness touched her deeply. "Thank you, Mother, but I think you might be getting a bit ahead of things. Come, let's sit down—I have something unpleasant to tell you." Taking her mother's arm, Kitty led her to a nearby bench. It had been one of Elizabeth's favorite spots for summer reading. Now, its stone facade was adorned with ivy vines, nature slowly reclaiming what man had built.

"Well, I'm seated now, so out with it. What is your unpleasant news?" Mrs. Bennet demanded, her impatience clear as she looked at her daughter.

Kitty had thought about this during her walk from Meryton, carefully considering where to begin explaining everything to her mother. In the end, she decided to start with the most pressing matter. "Well, Mother, I need you to know that there will be no wedding."

"What? Did you break it off with Mr. Tiffin as well? I must say, you are a very inconstant girl!"

"No, Mama, the engagement was never real."

Kitty saw the confusion in her mother's eyes and rushed to explain. "I asked Isaac Tiffin to pretend to be my fiancé because I needed to get rid of Mr. Blackwell."

"Mr. Blackwell? The one your father said was arrested for kidnapping?"

Kitty nodded. "Yes, that's him."

Mrs. Bennet sighed dramatically. "What a shame. He was such a handsome man. To think such an evil heart could be housed in such a beautiful frame. He must have loved you very much to commit a crime just to win your hand."

Kitty swallowed hard as panic surged within her. She thought of Isaac, beaten and drowning under a bridge. There was nothing remotely loving about the motivation for such an atrocity. "No, he didn't want me. He wanted my dowry."

"But you have no dowry!" her mother exclaimed.

"Mr. Blackwell thought I had a dowry because I lied to Lydia and told her I had one. He must have heard about it from her and came looking for a wife to fill his coffers."

"Why would you lie about a dowry? All along, you've insisted that you didn't want to marry, that you wanted to stay at home and care for your parents in their old age."

"Because," Kitty said, wringing her hands before her, "that too was a lie. I've always wanted to marry. I only said I didn't because I've been overlooked too many times to believe I could catch a man's eye. It hurts to be the invisible Bennet sister, so I lied and said I didn't want to marry."

Mrs. Bennet eyed her daughter as though really seeing her for the first time. "You have had a rough time of it, being the last girl at home. I can see that now. But take heart—you caught Mr. Tiffin's eye. Fake engagement or no, it's clear as the nose on his face that he fancies you."

Kitty smiled sadly. "He is the most honorable man I have ever known, Mama. I hold him in the highest esteem."

"What do you want, Kitty? Be honest with yourself now. What is your heart telling you?"

Kitty didn't need to think long. She knew what her heart wanted because it screamed at her every moment of the day. "I want Isaac. I wish more than anything that the fake romance was real."

Mrs. Bennet smiled, patting Kitty's tightly clasped hands with one of her own. "Then let's make it real."

❧❧❧❧❧ ❦❦❦❦❦

Isaac Tiffin wasn't known as a man prone to nervousness. He had always considered himself steady—an unmovable rock lashed by the storm winds of life. Yet today, he was nothing but nervous. He paced as he dressed, taking extra care with his simply tied cravat. At breakfast, he mumbled to himself enough to make his hosts exchange amused smiles over their eggs. Twice, he started out the door—once forgetting his watch entirely. Outside the Phillips townhouse, Isaac began walking, stopped, and returned to the front gate no fewer than three times, his courage faltering the farther he ventured from its safety.

And yet, terrified as he was—and he was terrified—Isaac knew his purpose that morning was a noble one. Resolving himself, he figuratively shook his fearful heart, steadied his resolve, and set off toward the outskirts of town and Longbourn.

As he walked, he reflected on all that had brought him to this moment: a terrible accident on a Cumbrian lake, a kind grandmother who took him in and raised him; her wish for a greater life than that of a farmer for her grandson; his journey to Meryton and his disastrous failure as a law clerk. And most of all... Catherine Bennet.

Before he knew it, Isaac was knocking on Longbourn's front door and being ushered in by a smug butler. The butler said nothing, merely taking his hat and leading him into the drawing room, where the entire Bennet family sat expectantly.

He entered, greeting Mrs. Bennet first, then Catherine, and finally Mr. Bennet, all while barely aware of what he was saying. Isaac only hoped he wasn't stumbling over his words, but the moment his eyes found Catherine, they caught on the sight of her downturned face. Everything else faded away. He saw only the slight smile on her lips and the blush painting her cheeks. Heavens, she was beautiful.

"Mr. Bennet," Mrs. Bennet interjected, taking her husband by the arm, "I require your advice on a matter in the dining room." To Isaac, she added, "We won't be but a moment. Kitty, do entertain our guest."

Isaac barely noticed as the elder Bennets left the room, their departure punctuated by the soft click of the door. His focus remained fixed on Catherine, though her words seemed to reach him as if from a distance.

"My apologies," he said, realizing he had missed what she'd said. "Could you repeat that?" Isaac swallowed the lump in his throat and took a steadying breath.

"I asked after your health," Catherine replied with a shy smile. "How goes your recovery?"

"Recovery?" Isaac echoed, his brow furrowing. "From what?"

"From your injuries incurred during your abduction."

Her eyes sparkled with a playful humor, and the sight of it sent a wave of warmth spreading across Isaac's chest.

"'Twas only a bit of fever and a few bruises. I'm right as rain now," Isaac replied, rocking back slightly on his heels. The mixture of joy and terror he felt was almost overwhelming.

Silence filled the space between them, heavy and oppressive, drap-ing itself over Isaac's shoulders until he feared he might never find his voice again.

It was Catherine who finally broke the stillness. "Is there a partic-ular reason for your visit today? Perhaps something I might assist you with?"

"No reason," Isaac blurted instinctively, immediately wincing at his own response. It was an obvious untruth, and the absurdity of it only deepened his discomfort.

Catherine laughed—a bright, musical sound that Isaac wanted to keep tucked in his coat pocket to take out on rainy days. "Mr. Tiffin, I do believe you just lied to me," she teased, her voice laced with playful mockery, her eyes alight with good humor.

"I believe you are right," Isaac admitted, his awkwardness melting away at last. "And I fear I learned the art of falsehood from you. There are moments, I've discovered, when a well-meaning untruth serves better than the plainest truth. Just yesterday, it helped me mend a family's broken heart over a misunderstanding. For that, I owe you my gratitude."

"It seems we've taught each other well," Catherine replied, her tone softer now. "Your honest nature made me want to be a better person, while my occasional dishonesty encouraged you to see the value in tempering truth with compassion."

Isaac reached out, gently taking her hands in his. Her fingers were delicate and warm, a perfect fit against his own. "Catherine Bennet," he began, his voice steady but filled with emotion, "I would like noth-ing more than to spend the rest of my life learning from you. Will you do me the honor of becoming my wife?"

He looked into her face, watching the moment the question registered. The light of joy flared in her lovely blue eyes, transforming them into something breathtaking.

"I will, Isaac Tiffin," Catherine said softly, her eyes alight with affection. "I should like nothing more than to continue learning honesty from you. I cannot think of a more pleasant existence."

Leaning down, Isaac closed the distance between them. He brushed his lips against hers, feeling, at last, that he had found his true place in the world.

EPILOGUE

It wasn't long before the Bennet breakfast table welcomed a new member. Mr. Tiffin arrived early to dine with his soon-to-be family and his recent employer, taking a seat beside where he knew Catherine Bennet would sit. The spot next to Kitty, once Lydia's, was now increasingly seen as Isaac's rightful place among them.

Kitty was usually the next to enter, motivated to rise early and dress quickly. Nothing like a beau to make a girl primp with haste. She had made it her habit to enter the dining room as though not seeing him. "Why, Mr. Tiffin, what a lovely surprise," she would always say, always drawing a smile from her betrothed.

"And what a lovely lady to surprise," he would invariably reply.

Kitty would then take her seat, and they would exchange shy glances until the rest of the family took their places at the table.

Mr. Bennet was next, no longer eager to read his newspaper. He would nod at Isaac, smile at his daughter, and then sit at the head of the table to preside over the morning meal.

This particular morning was much like the rest, with Mr. Bennet offering a brief greeting before diving directly into a discussion of the estate's affairs with his newly hired steward.

Longbourn had quickly benefited from Isaac's practical touch in the short time he had been working there. From the day he moved into the steward's cottage, he had taken it upon himself to visit every tenant in turn, including the Preece brothers, bringing with him enough paper to take down a list of issues with each property.

He had then traveled the entire length of the Longbourn estate with a sheaf of paper, taking detailed notes on what needed attention within the estate's boundaries. Isaac had proved himself diligent and thorough, traits Kitty knew her father prized.

"No talking business at the breakfast table!" chided Mrs. Bennet as she entered the dining room in a cloud of lavender water and lace.

"Of course, dear," Mr. Bennet replied in his usual dry tone. Kitty had noted a distinct increase in her father's patience with the family since Isaac had joined their little unit. She supposed it was largely because he had fewer worries about the estate to ponder, or perhaps it was because he was generally happier to have a male member of the family to converse with.

Kitty knew that her father had always wanted a son, which was why he had gravitated more toward Elizabeth, whose quick wit and abundant intelligence would have made her the ideal heir, had she had the foresight to be born with the right gender.

Now her father had a potential son-in-law who would be living nearby and who seemed genuinely interested in the affairs of Longbourn in a way that Mr. Bingley and Mr. Darcy, as masters of their own estates, could never be. By proposing to Kitty, Isaac had unintentionally fulfilled the dreams of more than one of the members of the Bennet household.

"Good morning, Mama," Kitty rang out. "Did you sleep well?" She asked, hoping to stave off a family squabble. It was best to focus her mother's attention on the things she liked most to speak about...namely, herself.

"Oh, I had the most dreadful night," Mrs. Bennet said happily as she sat between Mr. Bennet and his daughter. "Such aches and pains I had! I felt as if my back were broken in two. I tell you, Kitty, the maid is laying iron rods in my bed to keep me up at night, I just know it!"

"I will speak to her if you wish, Mama," Kitty said, smiling at Isaac, who exchanged a knowing glance with her.

Isaac had filled a plate with what he had begun to call "Catherine's Adventure," a breakfast plate of ham, eggs, buttered toast, and a cup of blueberries. Setting the plate before her, he gave her a wink. He poured her a coffee next, sweetened with sugar and lightened with cream.

How she loved this man, Kitty thought, sipping from the steaming cup. He saw her in a way no one else had. Lydia's shadow was finally stepping into the sunshine, walking beside the man she loved. Everything felt brighter, warmer, because of Isaac Tiffin.

She no longer had to lie about the life she led, for reality was far better than anything she could have imagined. As her mother chattered, her father quipped, and her fiancé chuckled, Kitty Bennet felt that this was the best ending for any Bennet sister. She would be the one to stay at Longbourn, to watch over her parents, and eventually, to have a family of her own. Her dreams had come true—all of them—and all because of a lie.

ABOUT THE AUTHOR

AMANDA ORNECK was raised in Southern California on a healthy diet of captivating stories, so she grew up always knowing she wanted to be a writer. She wrote her first story at the age of five and began her first novel at eleven. While attaining a Bachelor's in Creative Writing from USC, Amanda received the Middleton Fellowship for excellence in Poetry. Today she is the published author of several novels and short stories. She currently lives in Toney, Alabama, where she spends her days gardening, reading, and loving her family to pieces.

EXCERPT FROM THE FRONT PORCH SUPPER CLUB

COMING SPRING 2025

Now was his chance. If Luke wanted to show he could manage the Hospitality Division of the Ballard Hotel Group, what better way than to help its biggest resort project today find the perfect building site. "I have an idea of a site that would be perfect for this project."

"Ideas don't exactly balance the data sheets, little brother," smirked his sister. Penelope knew she had him cornered. "We need to base our decisions on what will bring the most guest satisfaction, not on hunches."

"It sounds like you have everything under control, Penelope," said their father, the hint of a smile on his face. "If we don't have any further business, I'll adjourn this meeting until next week. Thank you all for coming." He stood up, shutting down Luke's unspoken retort.

The company directors all filed out of the conference room, with Penny strutting down the table like a proud peacock. Luke straightened his back as he stood from the chair. He refused to let her see weakness.

He made his way to his suite of offices, where his secretary Allison was waiting with his messages and his lunchtime nutrition shake." Robert Garcia from Menu Development called to say he's completed his termination meetings with all those we are letting go from his division. He just finished meeting with the last chef this morning."

There, see? Luke was efficient, his team did their work with premium quality, and he would make his rebranding target. He would show his sister and his father that he was more than they thought he was.

Luke snatched the bottle from her hands, saying "I'm going outside for lunch."

"Of course, sir," Allison responded, and handed him his earbud case. She knew that more often than not Luke would need to walk off his post-meeting frustration after meeting the weekly company head briefing.

"Thank you, Allison, do not forward calls to my cell." Luke handed her his tablet in exchange for the ear buds and headed toward the elevators.

On the elevator ride down to the lobby, Luke practiced his breathing exercises. In...pause and hold...out. By the time he was striding through the lobby toward the green space in the back of the building, Luke was able to project calm, even if he didn't feel it. Never would it be said that Luke Ballard couldn't keep his cool.

He avoided the revolving door as he didn't want to halt his progress, instead opting to use the regular set of glass doors beside it. Flipping open the earbud case, he popped one into his ear, pulled out the second, and shoved the case in his pocket. On his phone he tabbed over to Spotify to listen to the latest episode of the Coaching for Leaders podcast. He leaned over to put in the second earbud when he heard it: An ear-curdling scream.

It didn't sound like someone was being attacked, rather it was a scream of frustration, of rage, of an anger Luke desperately identified with in that moment. He wanted to find the owner of that scream and commiserate with them. Maybe they could do some screaming together.

Stepping into the perfectly manicured greenspace behind the Ballard building, Luke heard the sound of arguing just past the trees. As he approached, he saw a woman railing against the Founder's Tree that stood in the center of the green space. She was constantly moving, pacing, her arms flailing and alternating pulling at her short strawberry blond hair until it stood on end.

"How could they do this to me? I'm a graduate of the Institute of Culinary Education! Ugh!" The woman leaped into the air like a gazelle, and Luke leaned against one of the trees ringing the mound where the Founder's Tree stood. He could feel a smile pulling at his lips, but he tried to suppress it. It wouldn't be polite to laugh at someone else's pain, no matter how charming that someone might be when they yelled.

"I'll show you authentic!" She charged up the hill and threw a punch. It landed squarely against the trunk of the magnolia tree, which barely vibrated from the impact. She certainly felt it though, because she cried out, dropped to the ground, and stuck her knuckles in her mouth.

Alarmed, Luke dashed up the hill, dropping to his knees beside her. "Here, let me look at that." Gently as he could, he pulled her hand away from her mouth, noting the surprised look in her bright blue eyes.

"Who?" She managed to say through her shock and pain.

"Luke," he said as he inspected her hand. Two of the fingers seemed to be bruised and there was a nasty cut along her knuckles. Luke pulled a Band-Aid from his pocket first aid kit and applied it to the wound. "There you go." He picked up the wrappers from the bandage and folded them neatly before returning them and the first aid kit to his front pocket.

"Does Luke always carry a first aid kit?" She seemed more curious than pained, which was a good sign.

"He does when he leaves the house. He's always prepared, which means he can help people like...?" He let the word draw out and tilted his head in inquiry.

"Ruby."

"Which means he can help people like Ruby. She shouldn't go around punching trees, you know, especially not that one. The company founder brought that magnolia directly from his home in Alabama when they started construction on this building fifteen years ago."

Ruby's expression darkened. "The company, right. How did such a nice guy end up working for such an awful company as this?"

Luke smiled, though the slight against his family's legacy made his stomach sour. "How do you know I'm nice?"

Ruby said nothing, only held up her bandaged knuckles.

Luke decided it was best to ignore the question for now. He didn't think she'd like his answer much. Instead, he voiced his curiosity. "Why were you arguing with the Founder's Tree?"

"Because" Ruby said, heaving a huge sigh, "I just got fired because some pencil-neck stick-in-the-mud decided that my food wasn't 'authentic' enough." She had brought out the air quotes to emphasize the phrase "Authentic" but then winced when her knuckles objected.

Luke barely noticed her pain because now it was his turn to be good and angry. "Pencil-neck stick-in-the-mud?" What was this, 1956? Nobody insulted Luke Ballard, unless it was his sister.

Realization dawned and Ruby's eyes spit fire. "So you're the pencil-neck, aren't you? I hope you get food poisoning from all that authentic cuisine you love so much!"

She stomped down the hill and had reached the ring of trees when she stopped and came back up to him. "Can I please have another Band-Aid?"

Confused, Luke pulled out his first-aid kit and handed her another one.

"Thanks. Rebrand this!" She declared as she ran past him and punched the tree with the other hand. Then she screamed in pain, glared daggers and him, and walked away.

Follow me on Facebook to keep up to date on all my writing news: https://www.facebook.com/amanda.orneck.author

ALSO BY AMANDA ORNECK

Romance
Mary's Song—A Pride and Prejudice *Variation*
Science Fiction
Deus Hex Machina: Sister of the Circuit

Out of Print
Shadow of the Owl